HELL PASO

Morgan Latimer is a drifter, riding through the West trying to escape his past, and especially trouble. During his travels, he is forced to take shelter in a cave as a massive dirt storm plunges him into darkness. After it passes, Latimer overhears a scuffle breaking out between a man and a woman at a nearby creek. Not one to sit back and watch a woman be assaulted, he intervenes — and immediately realizes he has found the trouble he was trying to avoid . . .

740009715227

MATT COLE

HELL PASO

Complete and Unabridged

LINFORD
Leicester

First published in Great Britain in 2016 by
Robert Hale
an imprint of The Crowood Press
Wiltshire

First Linford Edition
published 2019
by arrangement with
The Crowood Press
Wiltshire

A catalogue record for this book is available
from the British Library.

ISBN 978–1–4448–4010–0

Published by
F. A. Thorpe (Publishing)
Anstey, Leicestershire

Set by Words & Graphics Ltd.
Anstey, Leicestershire
Printed and bound in Great Britain by
T. J. International Ltd., Padstow, Cornwall

This book is printed on acid-free paper

Hell in Texas

The devil, we're told,
in hell was chained,
And a thousand years
he there remained;
He never complained nor
did he groan,
But determined to start a hell
of his own,
Where he could torment the
souls of men
Without being chained in
a prison pen.
So he asked the Lord
if he had on hand
Anything left when he made
the land.

The Lord said, 'Yes,
I had plenty on hand,
But I left it down on
the Rio Grande;

The fact is, old boy,
the stuff is so poor
I don't think you could use it in
hell anymore.'
But the devil went down to look
at the truck,
And said if it came as a gift he
was stuck;
For after examining it
carefully and well
He concluded the place was too
dry for hell.

So, in order to get it
off his hands,
The Lord promised the devil to
water the lands;
For he had some water,
or rather some dregs,
A regular cathartic that smelled
like bad eggs.
Hence the deal was closed and
the deed was given
And the Lord went back to
his home in heaven.
And the devil then said,

'I have all that is needed
To make a good hell,'
and hence he succeeded.

He began to put thorns in all of
the trees,
And mixed up the sand with
millions of fleas;
And scattered tarantulas
along all the roads;
Put thorns on the cactus and
horns on the toads.
He lengthened the horns
of the Texas steers,
And put an addition on
the rabbit's ears;
He put a little devil in the
broncho steed,
And poisoned the feet of
the centipede.

The rattlesnake bites you,
the scorpion stings,
The mosquito delights you
with buzzing wings;
The sand-burrs prevail

and so do the ants,
And those who sit down need half
soles on their pants.
The devil then said that
throughout the land
He'd managed to keep up the
devil's own brand,
And all would be mavericks
unless they bore
The marks of scratches and bites
and thorns by the score.

The heat in the summer is
a hundred and ten,
Too hot for the devil and too hot
for men.
The wild boar roams through
the black chaparral, —
It's a hell of a place he
has for a hell.
The red pepper grows
on the banks
of the brook;
The Mexicans use it in all
that they cook.
Just dine with a Greaser and

4

then you will shout,
'I've hell on the inside as well
as the out!'

— Unknown

1

The drifter was riding just below the peak of the ridge, occasionally elevating his head so as to stare across the crest, shading his eyes with one hand to thus better concentrate his vision. Both horse and rider unmistakably exhibited signs of exhaustion, but every movement of the latter showed perpetual watchfulness, his glance roving the barren ridges, a brown Winchester lying cocked across the saddle pommel, his left hand taut on the rein. Thus far, the horse he bestrode barely required restraint, advancing slowly, with head hanging low, and only occasionally breaking into a brief trot under the thrust of the spur.

The rider — Morgan Latimer — was a man approaching his mid-thirties, rather lean and long of limb, but possessing broad, squared shoulders above a deep chest, sitting the saddle easily in plainsman style, yet with an erectness of carriage which suggested military training. The face under the wide brim of the weather-worn slouch hat was clean-shaven, browned by sun and wind, and powerfully marked, the chin somewhat prominent, the mouth fixed, the gray eyes full of character and daring. His dress was that of rough service, plain leather chaps showing marks of hard usage, a gray woolen shirt turned low at the neck, with a handkerchief knotted loosely about the sinewy-bronzed throat. At one hip dangled the holster of a .44, on the other hung a canvas-covered canteen. His was a figure and face to be noted anywhere, a man from whom you would expect both thought and action, and one who seemed to exactly fit into the wild surroundings in which he rode through.

Where he rode was the very western extreme of the prairie country, billowed like the sea, and from off the crest of its higher ridges, the wide level sweep of the plains was noticeable, extending like a vast brown ocean to the foothills of the far away mountains. Yet the actual beginning of that drear, barren stretch was fully ten miles distant, while all about where he rode the conformation was irregular, comprising narrow valleys and swelling mounds, with here and there a sharp ravine, river from the rock, and invisible until one drew up startled at its very brink. The general trend of depression was undoubtedly southward, leading toward the valley of the Rio Grande, yet unbalanced ridges occasionally cut across, adding to the confusion. The entire surrounding landscape presented the same aspect. There was no special object upon which the eye could rest for guidance; there was no tree, no upheaval of rock, no uniqueness of summit, no snake-like trail . . . all about extended the same dull, dead monotony of brown, sun-baked hills, with slightly greener depressions lying between, interspersed by patches of sand or the white gleam of alkali. It was a dreary, deserted land, parched under the hot summer sun, brightened by no vegetation, excepting sparse bunches of buffalo grass or an occasional stunted sage bush, and disclosing nowhere the slightest sign of human habitation.

The rising sun reddened the crest of the hills, and the rider, halting his willing horse, sat motionless, gazing securely into the southwest. Apparently, he observed nothing there unusual, for he slowly turned his body about in the saddle, sweeping his eyes, inch by inch, along the line of the horizon, until the entire circuit had been completed. Then his flattened lips smiled slightly, his hand unconsciously patting the horse's neck.

'I reckon we're still alone, old girl,' he said quietly. He spoke in the soft accents of the North, and yet his speech was colored with just a trace of his Northern birth — a musical drawl seldom heard far from that portion of

Texas bordering the Rio Bravo del Norte. 'We'll try for the trail, and take it easy.'

The horse snorted in reply.

He swung stiffly out of the saddle, and with reins dangling over his shoulder, began the slower advance on foot, the exhausted horse trailing behind. His was not a situation in which one could feel certain of safety, for any ridge might conceal the wary foemen he sought to avoid, yet he proceeded now with renewed confidence. It was summer time, and the place the very heart of the Indian country, with every separate tribe ranging between the Yellowstone and the Brazos and beyond, either restless or openly on the warpath. Rumors of atrocities were being retold the length and breadth of the border, and every report drifting in to either fort or settlement only added to the alarm. For once at least the Plains Indians had discovered a common cause, tribal differences had been adjusted in war against the white invader, and the Kiowas, Comanches, Arapahoes, Cheyennes, and the Sioux had become welded together in savage brotherhood. To oppose them were the scattered and unorganized settlers lining the more eastern streams, guarded by small detachments of regular troops posted here and there amid that broad wilderness, scarcely within touch of each other.

Everywhere beyond these lines of patrol wandered roaming war parties, attacking travelers on the trails, raiding exposed settlements, and occasionally venturing to try open battle with the small squads of armed men. In this stress of sudden emergency — every available soldier on active duty — civilians had been pressed into service, and hastily dispatched to warn exposed settlers, guide wagon trains, or carry dispatches between outposts. And thus the rider, who knew every foot of the plains lying between the Mississippi and the Rio Grande Rivers, was one of those suddenly drifting, merely because he chanced to be involved in the plights of others. His good-natured being had been involved with or created too much trouble.

Thus some weeks later, he was riding swiftly into the southwest, trying desperately to outrun his past and his troubles. To the drifter this had been merely another page in a life of adventure, of running, of trying to find peace; for him to take his life in his hands had long ago become an old story. He had quietly performed the special duty allotted him, watched a squadron of troopers trot forth down in too many battles, received the hasty thanks of the peppery little generals and captains. Then, having nothing better to do, traded his horse in at the government corral for a fresh mount, a beautiful strawberry roan that he immediately knew he would have for the rest of their lives.

He then started back again through Texas. For the greater portion of two nights and a day, he had been in the saddle, but he was accustomed to this, for he had driven more than one bunch of longhorns up the Texas trail. As he had slept a few hours at Fort Bliss, and as his nerves were like steel, the thought of danger gave him slight concern. He was thoroughly tired, and it rested him to get out of the saddle, while the freshness of the morning air was a tonic, the very breath of which made him forgetful of fatigue.

After all, this was indeed the very sort of experience which appealed to him, and always had — this life of peril in the open, under the stars and the sky. He had constantly experienced it for so long now, nearly eight years, as to make it seem merely natural. While he ploughed steadily forward through the shifting sand of the coulee, his thoughts drifted idly back over those years, and sometimes he smiled, and occasionally glowered, as various incidents returned to memory. It had been a turbulent life, yet one not unusual to those of his generation.

There was much not over pleasant to remember, and those strenuous years of almost ceaseless fighting, of long night marches, of swift, merciless raiding, of lonely scouting within the enemy's lines, of severe wounds, hardship, and loves lost and of suffering, had left their marks on both body and soul.

What an utter waste it all seemed, now that he looked back upon it. Over seven years of fighting, hardship, and rough living, and what had they brought him? The reputation of a hard rider, a daring player at cards, a quick shot, a skilled horseman, a man who scorned danger, and a bad man to fool with — that was the whole of a record hardly won.

Nonetheless, he was a man who wanted peace. A man who wanted to find a place where he could avoid trouble and just rest.

The man's eyes hardened, his lips set firmly, as this truth came crushing home. A pretty life story, surely, one to be proud of, and with probably no better ending than an Indian bullet, or the flash of a revolver in some bar room fight.

The narrow valley along which he was travelling suddenly changed its direction, compelling him to climb the rise of the ridge. Slightly below the summit, he halted. In front extended the wide expanse of the Mesa Valley, a scene of splendor under the golden rays of the sun, with vivid contrast of colors, the gray of rocks, the yellow of sand, the brown of distant hills, the green of flora, and the silver sheen of the stream half-hidden behind the border of cottonwoods lining its banks.

This was a sight Morgan Latimer had often looked upon, but not always with appreciation, and for the moment, his eyes swept across from bluff to bluff without thought except for its wild beauty. Then he perceived something, which instantly startled him into attention — yonder, close beside the river, just beyond that ragged bunch of cottonwoods, slender spirals of dark clouds were visible. That would hardly be a thunderstorm during the long summer months in Texas at this hour of the day, and besides, the trail along here ran close in against the bluff, coming down to the river at the ford two miles further west. No party of plainsmen would ever venture to build a fire in so exposed a spot, and no small company would take the chances of the trail. Surely, that appeared to be the flap of a canvas wagon top a little to the right of the smoke, yet all was so far away he could not be certain. He stared in that direction a long while, shading his eyes with both hands, unable to decide. There were three or four moving black dots higher up the river, but so far away he could not distinguish whether they were men or animals. Only as outlined against the yellow sand dunes could he tell they were advancing westward toward the ford.

Decidedly bewildered by all this, yet

resolute to solve the mystery and unwilling to remain hidden there until night, the drifter led his horse along the slant of the ridge, until he attained a sharp break through the bluff leading down into the valley. It was a rugged gouge, nearly impassable, but a half hour of toil won them the lower prairie, the winding path preventing the slightest view of what might be meanwhile transpiring below. Once safely out in the valley the river could no longer be seen, while barely a hundred yards away, winding along like a great serpent, ran the deeply rutted trail through Texas. In neither direction appeared any sign of human life. As near as he could determine from those distant cottonwoods outlined against the sky, for the spirals in the sky were growing thicker by then to be observed, the spot sought must be considerably to the right of where he had emerged. With this idea in mind, he advanced cautiously, his every sense alert, searching anxiously for fresh signs of passage or evidence of a wagon train having deserted the beaten track, and turned south.

2

For the tenth time in just about ten minutes, a big man named Obadiah Duke stepped on his father's heels as they made their furtive way along the broken-backed ridges above Willow Creek in the Mesa Valley.

The rangeland was at its unpicturesque worst. For two days, the wind had raged and ranted over the hilltops, and whooped up the long coulees, so that tears stood in the eyes of the Duke men when they faced it; impersonal tears blown into being by the very force of the wind. Also, when they faced it they rode with bodies aslant over their saddle-horns and hats pulled low over their streaming eyes, and with coats fastened jealously close. If there were buttons enough, well and good; if not, a strap cinched tightly about the middle was considered pretty lucky and not to be despised.

The violent, ill-tempered old man, father of the other men, stopped, bringing the clan to a halt. He glowered aggressively, and his dry, harsh voice was mixed with sarcasm as he asked, 'Ain't you fergot somethin', son?'

The hulking Obadiah, second of Clifton Duke's four boys, was wary. He didn't like questions, mostly because he could never figure them out. That was the sole reason he quit school. Even amongst the Dukes, not noted through El Paso County for their immense intellects, large, brawny Obadiah was regarded as a touch slower than the rest of the clan.

'What?' he grunted. 'What I *fergot*?'

'Your thick glasses,' Clifton replied harshly.

'What?'

'And your walking stick.'

Obadiah scratched the side of his head with the foresight of his hunting rifle. He could not make sense of this conversation.

It was very dark, and the wind was increasing. The last gust had been preceded by an ominous roaring down the whole mountainside, which continued for some time after the trees in the little valley had lapsed into silence. The air was filled with a faint, cool, sodden odor, as of stirred forest depths. In those intervals of silence, the darkness seemed to increase in proportion and grow almost palpable. Yet out of this sightless and soundless void now came the tinkle of a spur's rowels, the dry crackling of saddle leathers, and the muffled plunge of a hoof in the thick carpet of dust and desiccated leaves. The youngest of Clifton Duke's sons wasn't getting the irony of the situation.

'My walking stick, Dad?' he mumbled softly. 'Huh?'

'And a tin cup for your pencils,' the mean old man chipped in, tugging the brim of his floppy brown hat lower over his eyes and squirting a stream of blackish tobacco juice at an inoffensive and harmless plant. 'That's what's bothering me, where are your pencils and your walkin' stick and your goddamned thick glasses?'

Although all of the Duke offspring, with the exception of daughter Alma, were bigger than their runt of a father, they were all cautious of him — and for good reason. Clifton Duke's tongue could strip the flesh off a dead buffalo. Compared to this old hill man, a badger had an even temperament. People claimed that the tobacco juice he spat from his twisted old mouth would paralyze a timber rattlesnake — things like that. He often made life unreasonably uncomfortable for his four large sons, and right now, it was Obadiah's turn.

Obadiah knew he was in trouble, but couldn't quite figure out why or how as he stood in the silvery moonlight staring into his father's face, as though hopeful of finding a clue amongst the hair on his leathery face.

All the same, he didn't. And Clifton Duke wasn't about to offer any assistance. That duty fell to his brother Grant, who cupped a hand to Obadiah's big ear and whispered, 'He's sayin' that you are blind as a *bat*.'

Obadiah stared back with a confused look. 'Why?'

'You don't know?' the father of the boys asked harshly.

Obadiah couldn't even manage that. Stalking along the ridges under the big old Texas moon in search of his sister and the man with whom she'd been seen sneaking off with towards the river, Obadiah had been enjoying himself so much that he was not even aware he'd been trampling all over the back of his father's feet.

★　★　★

Grant had explained as if addressing a child. Obadiah pouted, and then looked incensed. All this commotion over something so unimportant when their one and only sister might — at that very moment — be surrendering her fair pale body into the arms of some no-good man, he thought. It was time, he decided, to make a stand.

'Sometimes, Dad,' his voice rumbled from his toes, 'you gets to carryin' on like you ain't real sure that you are my daddy or my mommy.'

There was a surprised intake of breath from Grant, Clayton, and Levi as their old man went stiff. The Duke boys had to be careful when mentioning their mother, who had run off with one of the ranch hands from the Golden Plume Ranch years earlier. Maybe Obadiah had gone too far.

Clifton Duke certainly thought so. Depositing his long rifle against the trunk of a twisted tree, he spat copiously, snorted, and then adopting the classical prizefighter's stance raised his crooked fists and said, 'Put up or shut up, boy!'

This was nothing new. Ever since Grant, the oldest, had outgrown his father at around the age of thirteen, Clifton Duke had been fearful of his sons getting the edge on him, so he often challenged them to test themselves against him.

His challenges were never accepted. Any one of his boys could have whipped the pants off their dad, but they feared the aftermath of such a victory might consist of a sneak attack by their father or a bullet in their back.

'Dad!' chided Clayton, stepping in between his father and his brother. 'We don't have time to waste on this. There is a dirt storm comin'.'

'That boy has no respect!' Clifton Duke stated, still with his fists up. He knew that Clayton was right; they could see the spirals of dust clouds forming on the distant horizon to the East.

'What about Alma's honor?' demanded Levi, the youngest of the four boys. He then stepped closer and asked in a hushed tone, 'What iffen she's with a *Filmore*?'

This thought outraged them all; they hadn't thought of that until that moment. As protectors of their sister's fair name, they had responded immediately to the suspicion that buxom Alma may have snuck off to meet up with a beau tonight. That was bad enough, but the possibility that she might be seeing a Filmore — the Dukes' most bitter enemies in the area — was enough to jolt even a hard, stubborn man like Clifton Duke out of his desire to want to fight.

Clifton Duke straightened, thought for a moment, and then went for his rifle.

'That's not going to end well for the Filmore,' he said. He started off, and then stopped abruptly. 'Grant, you come with me.' He scowled at Obadiah. 'I don't think my feet can take any more of your trampling over them. We may have to find some cover if that storm moves any closer too.'

'Sorry,' Obadiah muttered. 'I cain't help it I'm so gull darned big.' It always paid to apologize to the old man. He could make your life a misery otherwise. Obadiah may have been slow, nevertheless, he was learning.

'And so you should be, you big ox,' shot back Clifton, never a man to accept an apology with grace. 'Maybe I should leave you out in the storm, knock some sense into you.'

That touched Obadiah off again.

'Oh yeah? Iffen I'm so big and dumb, how come it was me who figured Alma was up to no good tonight while the rest of you were sittin' around with a whiskey jug? Tell me that, Daddy.'

Clifton Duke scowled, yet try as he might, couldn't counter his son's statement. For it had been the slow and big Obadiah who'd caught the aroma of perfume on the night air at the Duke ranch and compound which had led to the discovery of three fluffed pillows in his sister's bed and the most damning evidence of all — Alma's missing blue dress.

'Just don't tread on nobody else, OK?' was the best the old man could come up with, and shouldering his rifle, led the way along the clear sign of

28

Alma's footprints in the Texas soil. 'The trail is going to disappear iffen that storm passes over us.'

They spurred forward in silence. It was not long before the wayside trees began to dimly show spaces between them, and the ferns to give way to lower, thick-set shrubs, which in turn yielded to a velvety moss, with long quiet intervals of netted and tangled grasses.

A short distance farther on, a trail abruptly swung off a ridge and angled down through the Sassafras trees in the direction of Willow Creek.

Clifton and his sons exchanged sober glances.

It seemed their worst fears were well founded.

The banks of Willow Creek, especially on a moonlit night, were well known as a meeting place for young lovers with some really serious courting in mind.

There was a storm coming and it wasn't made of dust and dirt, but this one was full of hatred, ignorance, and anger in the form of the Duke men.

3

Let us close our game of poker, take
our tin cups in our hand
As we all stand by the
cook's tent door
As dried mummies of hard crackers
are handed to each man.
O, hard tack, come again no more!
'Tis the song, the sigh of the hungry:
'Hard tack, hard tack,
come again no more.'
Many days you have lingered upon
our stomachs sore.
O, hard tack, come again no more!
'Tis a hungry, thirsty soldier who
wears his life away
In torn clothes — his better
days are o'er.
And he's sighing now for whiskey
in a voice as dry as hay,
'O, hard tack,
come again no more!' —

31

'Tis the wail that is heard in camp
both night and day.

The words, sung in a soft and musical tenor, died away and changed to a plaintive whistle, leaving the scene lonelier than ever. For a few moments, nothing was to be seen except the endless expanse of wilderness, and nothing was to be heard save the mournful warble of the singer. Then a horse and rider were suddenly framed where the sparse timber opened out upon the plain.

Together, man and mount made a striking picture; yet it would have been hard to say which was the more picturesque — the rider or the horse. The latter was a splendid beast, and its spotless hide of snowy white glowed in the rays of the afternoon sun. With bit chains jingling, it gracefully leaped a gully, landing with all the agility of a mountain lion, in spite of its enormous size.

The rider, still whistling his musical

tune, swung in the stock saddle as if he were a part of his horse. He was a lithe, lean young figure, dressed in fringed buckskin, touched here and there with the gray colors of the Southwest and of the Texas-Mexico borderland in which he rode.

His six-guns, wooden-handled, were suspended from a cartridge belt of carved leather, and hung low on each hip. His even teeth showed white against the deep sunburn of his face.

'Reckon we have to cut south,' he murmured to his horse. 'We haven't got any business in any towns, especially El Paso.'

* * *

Wheeling his mount, he searched the landscape with his keen blue eyes. Behind him was broken country; ahead of him was the terrible land that men called the Mesa Valley. The land rose to it in a long series of steppes with sharp ridges.

Queerly shaped and oddly colored buttes ascended toward it in a puzzling tangle. Dim in the distance was the country of Mexico itself — a mesa with a floor as even as a table; a treeless plain without even a weed or shrub for a landmark; a plateau of peril without end. It was different than the others he had passed, as if all life had died right here.

The rider was doing well to avoid any badlands, towns, any civilization in general. Outlaw Indian bands roamed over its desolate expanse — the only human beings who could live there. In the winter, snowstorms raced screaming across it, from Texas to New Mexico, for half a thousand miles. It was a country of extremes. In the summer, it was a scorching griddle of heat dried out by dry desert winds. Water was hard to find there, and food still harder to obtain. And it was now late summer — the season of mocking mirages and deadly sun.

The horseman was just about to turn his steed's head directly to the south-ward when a sound came to his ears — the sound of a storm whipping up fast. It was a dust storm — a wall of dirt amassing and heading his way. The clouds appeared on the horizons with a thunderous roar. Turbulent dust clouds rolled in very quickly. The electrical current in the air was so strong that it snapped from ear to ear on his strawberry roan.

The sand got pretty close to before the wind started. The front was just a few miles away when the wind got very strong. North winds whipped dust of the drought area to a new fury — blotting out every speck of light. The black, ominous cloud rolled over the plains from the north, an awe-inspiring spectacle.

A huge cloud of black top soil swooped down upon the land in the manner of a heavy cloud, flattening out upon the earth and spreading absolute darkness, the like of which he had heard but never experienced in such a manner before.

It was as though the sky was divided into two opposite worlds. On the south, there was blue sky, golden sunlight and tranquility; on the north face, there was a menacing curtain of boiling black dust that appeared to reach a thousand or more feet into the air. It had the appearance of a mammoth waterfall in reverse — color as well as form. The apex of the cloud was plumed and curling, seething and tumbling over itself from north to south and whipping shrubbery and foliage around like feathers in the wind.

Darkness settled swiftly after the drifter had been enveloped in the stinking, stinging dust. Breathing was extremely difficult for the drifter and his strawberry roan. The great cloud of dust rose a thousand feet into the air, blue gray. In front of it were six or seven whirling columns of dust, drifting up like cigar smoke.

The dust storm turned day into

night. 'It has made the sun disappear,' Morgan Latimer said to his great strawberry roan.

A great black bank rolled in out of the northeast, and in a twinkling when it struck, plunged everything into inky blackness, worse than that on any midnight, when there is at least some starlight and outlines of objects could be seen.

The drifter pondered a thought. When dust obscures sun, was it considered cloudy?

Morgan Latimer believed the world was coming to an end. The sky turned darker than a thunderstorm. Never had he been in such all-enveloping blackness before, such impenetrable gloom.

And then a blinding, rust-colored cloud blew into town with a vengeance.

Was this Texas, or Hell he was riding into?

There appeared to be thousands of frightened birds flying, rabbits running, and tumbleweeds blowing ahead of the dirt cloud. The drifter pulled his horse through the storm, trying to find a shelter.

As it approached, its face was a dark, rolling bank and the sunlight was completely shut out. Latimer literally touched his nose with his hand and could not see his hand. Within minutes, everything was dark, and the wind and dust were in his eyes so badly that he was having considerable trouble seeing anything at all.

It was so sudden of a storm. Dawn had come clear and rosy all across the plains that day. By noon the skies were so fresh and blue that the drifter thought he would reach New Mexico for sure before darkness had fallen.

He had been wrong.

He was used to having his heart broken and his dreams squashed, just not by a storm. This was the dust-storm country. It was the saddest land the drifter had ever seen.

It is so frightening and hard to breathe in this wind and the dust is so bad, the drifter thought.

In the dust-covered desolation of the western part of Texas here, the lean man wore his hat low, with his handkerchief tied over his face. The wind burned him — the wind and the gravel, it felt like it, burning his legs. It was hitting so hard on his legs before he was able to find shelter.

That was when he faintly made out the silhouette of a cave.

At least he hoped it was a cave.

4

It was a cave and a respectable one at that. It was high-roofed, airy, bone-dry and accommodating. More importantly, the cave provided the shelter he would need from the sudden blackness of the dust storm outside. The scars and ashes of old fires showed that it had seen frequent use in the past, and to the eyes of a somnolent man, it looked as inviting as any suite in the finest hotels in any big city. It was high enough he rode his horse in with him.

The drifter knew when those dust storms blew and a person was out in 'em, it would just coat the inside of his nose literally. And sometimes when he opened his mouth, it would just get cottony dry because, well, he was spitting out dirt sometimes. It looked like tobacco juice, only it was dirt, when he had spit. It was pretty awful. But

Latimer just thought that was part of living and traveling through parts of West Texas.

It had been high noon in the desert, but there was no dazzling sunlight now, just a world of whirling dirt and gravel. Over the earth hung a twilight, a yellow-pink softness that flushed across the sky like the approach of a shadow, covering everything yet concealing nothing, creeping steadily onward, yet seemingly still, until, pressing low over the earth, it took on changing colors, from pink to gray, gray to black — gloom that precedes tropical showers. Then the wind came — a breeze rising as it were from the hot earth — forcing an invisible dagger into his side, sending dust-devils swirling across the slow curves of the desert — and then the storm burst in all its might.

The cave's new inhabitants had covered close to fifty miles that day, riding through the New Mexico and now Texas country in his endless quest for the thing he found the hardest to find in life — peace.

Down the slopes to the west billowed giant clouds of sand. At the bottom, these clouds tumbled and surged and mounted, and then, resuming their headlong course, swept across the flat land bordering the river, hurtled across the swollen Rio Grande itself. And on up the gentle rise of ground to the town, where they swung through the streets in ruthless strides — banging signs, ripping up roofing, snapping off branches — and then lurched out over the mesa to the east. Here, as if in glee over their escape from city confines, they redoubled in fury and tore down to earth.

Latimer stood six foot three, lean as a coyote and an even-tempered man by his own rights, and was never sure just how a man like himself seemed to attract such trouble. He knew men who lived for trouble, who thrived on it, but never seemed to land in it half as much as he did. He had met prizefighters who'd had less conflict, gunfighters who had traded less lead, black-hearted riders of the dark trails and back alleys of boom towns who'd had fewer nights' rest interrupted by calamity and mayhem.

It just didn't make sense.

The storm whipped and howled past outside.

How could a man want something so badly, yet find it so hard to attain?

Was it possible — as a shady gypsy woman had once told him after checking out his rein-calloused hands — that he actually had been born beneath the sign of Mars — the god of war? And no matter how he tried to live his life he would find upheaval, friction, violence and turmoil wherever he roamed? Was he really a cursed man?

He smiled at that possibility now as he lowered his lanky frame into a relaxed, cross-legged position before his merry little fire.

Fortune telling was all so much hoopla, he assured himself, for hadn't he experienced only peace and fair weather all the way across the Texas countryside? And could he deny that not even one person had tried to punch him in the face or knock him off his horse since he'd decided to leave for New Mexico, passing through Texas a few weeks back?

He could not. The omens all indicated that Morgan Latimer's time of peace was at hand.

Latimer listened, noting each change in its velocity as told by the sound of raging gusts outside. Once he lifted a corner of the blanket and peered out — only to suffer the sting of a thousand needles. Again, he hunched his shoulders guardedly and endeavored to roll a cigarette; but the tempestuous blasts discouraged this also, and with a curse he dashed the tobacco from him. After that, he remained still, listening, until he heard an agreeable change outside. The screeching sank to a crooning; the crooning dropped to a low, musical sigh. Flinging off the blanket, he rose and swept the desert with eyes sand-filled and blinking.

The last of the yellow winds was eddying slowly past. All about him the air, thinning rapidly, pulsated in the early evening sun's rays, which, beaming mildly down upon the desert, were spreading everywhere in glorious sheen. To the east, the mountains, stepping forth in the clearing atmosphere, lay revealed in a warmth of soft purple while the slopes to the west, over which the storm had broken, shone in a wealth of dazzling yellow-white light — sunbeams scintillating off myriads of tiny sand cubes. The desert was itself again — bright, resplendent — gripped in the clutch of solitude.

Whistling a little song he had heard a while back to himself, Latimer — as he preferred to be called — stirred the beans in his cooking pot with a broom snakeweed twig, while less than 150 yards away, across slick-flowing Willow Creek, the peace of Willow Glen was being well and truly disturbed by a dark-haired man who was trying to persuade a strawberry blonde young woman that his intentions were strictly honorable.

'Alma, don't you trust me?' Ambrose Orton said.

'I did . . . that was before you tried to remove my dress, Ambrose.'

'God almighty, girl! That's just so we's can go swimmin'.' Ambrose was not understanding the woman's resistance. 'Least we can get all this dirt off us from the storm, can't we?'

'Well, if that was all you had in mind, that would be OK, but I think you have more in mind,' Alma Duke replied.

The couple was seated on a rough-hewn bench where lovers of Mission Valley and the nearby El Paso had been carving their names and plighting their troths for year. Ambrose Orton, a slick operator from the Golden Plume Ranch, was beginning to run out of patience. He had gone to a great deal of time and trouble and told a pack of lies to persuade Alma Duke to sneak out and meet him tonight, but seemed to be getting nowhere fast.

And he couldn't figure where he went wrong.

He considered himself quite the prize: tall, dark and handsome, usually with a way around the ladies. He just could not understand Alma's opposition, so he took time out to question her.

Grateful for breathing space, Alma tidied up her hair and shifted a little farther along the bench. Ambrose slid after her.

She said, 'It's my family, Ambrose.'

Ambrose Orton didn't quite understand. Of course he knew the Duke-Filmore feud which had given the El Paso area considerable notoriety over recent years, and knew that the Dukes were a harsh, quick-shooting clan of hill people whom some of the more respectable folks of El Paso regarded as sub-human. But he couldn't see how Alma's family could prevent them from getting together.

Actually, it was Ambrose's technique that was the real problem, but Alma was too polite to say that. Ambrose Orton belonged to the grab-'em-and-go-school of romance. Alma didn't mind being grabbed occasionally. Indeed, so strict had been the supervision imposed upon her after an hour's activities over the years by four suspicious and overly protective brothers and a tyrannical father, that she yearned for a really good grab just to keep her going. Unfortunately, it had taken only a few minutes with Ambrose Orton for her to realize he was definitely not her idea of a romantic lover. He was good-looking enough, but about as understated as a Texas tornado. She was prepared to use any excuse to bring the night to an end.

'I keep thinking they are going to pop up from behind the bushes,' she claimed. 'My brothers, I mean.'

'There ain't anybody out here but the two of us,' Ambrose shot back. 'That storm sure made a mess of the two of us, too. So why don't we just get undressed and cleaned up? Don't worry about your brothers and pa finding us out here. I'm sure they're tucked in back at the compound.'

'You don't know my brothers or my father.'

His arm went around her shoulders. 'I don't want to get to know them. I want to get to know you.'

'Do you have any idea what would happen if my brothers and my father saw us here, together?' Alma said with true alarm.

That made him pause. 'No, what would happen?'

'One of a couple of things.'

'Well, go on and tell 'em to me.'

'My father would either shoot you where you sit or force you to marry me,' Alma calmly said. 'Or worse, iffen he had the itching to . . . he might slit your throat or hang you from a nearby tree.'

Ambrose Orton stared. 'Nah, that

can't be right. People don't behave like that anymore. He's a ranch owner, not a barbarian.'

'You don't know my family,' Alma repeated. 'Especially my pa.'

'I said I don't want to know him. He sounds crazy as a loon,' the man said, pulling off his boots in hopes that Alma would start undressing.

He was determined to allow nothing to deter him tonight. In his eyes, Alma looked as luscious as a pear, ripe for the picking. And he wasn't about to allow discussion of her family to interfere with his fruit-plucking activities.

'We shouldn't be wasting time talking, especially about your brothers and father,' he said in what he thought to be a romantically husky voice. 'C'mon, show me how much you like me, Alma. I'm a good guy when you get to know me. How 'bout a kiss, Alma?'

Alma Duke resisted. Ambrose Orton returned his arm around her shoulders and squeezed tighter. She slapped him across his face. He laughed and he persisted as he tried to bury his face in the top of her dress. Alma then pushed him. Ambrose fell off the bench and his fingers were still clutching at her dress. There was a loud ripping sound and Alma leapt to her feet, trying to hold her dress on and keep her bosom from being exposed.

Discarding all pretense of subtlety, Ambrose Orton undid his belt and sprang at her, determined to have what he wanted; nothing else mattered.

Alma Duke turned and ran away with Ambrose Orton right on her heels. 'C'mon, Alma, quit playing hard to get!'

She was extremely troubled now, mad and alarmed too. For once, she almost wished her father and brothers were close by so they could intervene.

As Ambrose blocked the path leading away from the glen, she swerved, and the creek lay directly ahead. Alma made an instant decision and hoped it was the right one. Leaping from a smooth creek side boulder, she dove headlong into Willow Creek and swam strongly to the other side.

'Lord almighty, girl, shouldn't you have taken that dress off first before jumping into the river?'

Ambrose Orton hesitated, but only for a brief moment. Slipping out of the extravagant broadcloth coat he had worn especially in his attempt to impress Alma, he dove into the water and swam after her. He was a good swimmer, but made no headway on her who had been competing with her brothers at everything athletic all her life.

Alma held her lead right until she reached the far bank, and it was only then, as she made to clamber out, that she struck trouble. Her foot slipped on a wet stone and she tumbled into a deep pool. She looked over her shoulder. Ambrose was close and he was grinning like a wild animal approaching its wounded prey. Then, suddenly, his grin disappeared as something snaked over the girl's head and pushed him so hard in the forehead he went under.

Alma Duke blinked. Despite the water in her eyes and the uncertainty of the light, she realized that the 'something' had been the barrel of a Winchester rifle.

When she turned and looked up, she saw the weapon held in the firm hands of a very tall, lean man straddling the rocks above her.

'Need some help, ma'am?' the stranger asked, offering his hand. Then, as he hauled her effortlessly onto the rocks beside him, a spluttering Ambrose Orton came to the surface, only to be poked in the head hard again — a poke that had enough force to stop a raging longhorn.

'I don't know what to do about you, mister,' the lean man said, 'but whatever it is, you'd be better off on the other side of the creek before I get to make a decision that will not be in your favor.'

Ambrose Orton went under. When he

surfaced, he had swallowed a fair amount of Willow Creek to go along with all the dirt he had swallowed from the storm. His head rang like a thunderstorm, but he had enough sense left to turn around and head back to the other side. Flailing the water erratically, sputtering, half-choking and with every ardent fire thoroughly quenched, the valley's self-styled lover boy somehow made it back to the bank where he struggled out and turned to speak his mind.

But Alma Duke and the stranger with the rifle were gone.

5

Trembling powerfully, Alma Duke said, 'Don't look, mister.' She really didn't care if he looked. She was being a lady and presenting modesty.

'Morgan Latimer. You can call me Latimer. No, ma'am, I won't look. You just go right ahead and get yourself out of those wet clothes before you catch your death, and don't worry about me,' he said self-confidently.

Alma undressed and the flickering light of Morgan Latimer's fire glowed tenderly and touchingly over more of the Texas countryside that was made up of the sand, mesas, and scrub brush. Of course, the sand had been increased to the massive and sudden storm that had passed earlier.

Problem was, Latimer wasn't seeing these, either. He had given his word as a gentleman not to look. His eyes were closed and his back turned to the woman. A man wasn't worth anything if you couldn't trust his word.

Alma seized a blanket and draped it attractively around her naked frame. 'It's OK now; you can open your eyes, Mr Latimer.'

'Just Latimer,' he corrected, turning. He looked her over. She was a beautifully curvaceous young woman. He supposed he could hardly blame the character who had been swimming after her in the creek, even if he had seemed a bit overzealous. He moved closer to the fire. 'Coffee, ma'am?'

'Yes, thank you,' she replied.

The golden fire glow filled the case as they sat talking and sipping the steaming brew. Although by nature and circumstances inclined to be wary of strange males, Alma was quickly at ease in the tall stranger's company, easier perhaps than she should have been and more than she could ever remember having been with anybody else on such short acquaintance. For his part,

Latimer found her a nice, well-mannered, intelligent, and welcoming young woman. And from what he heard, she had a less than stellar family.

' . . . I snuck out tonight,' she openly admitted. 'I have to sneak out if I want to do anything. My pa is so protective and my brothers are . . . they mean well . . . they do, but . . . '

'I can see why they are with fellas like that one on the other side of the creek there,' Latimer noted.

'Ain't that the truth, but my pa believes all men are always up to no good,' Alma said. She looked at him and asked, 'Do you agree, Mr Latimer?'

'Most men are, for sure, ma'am,' Latimer said. He stirred the fire with a stick and felt its warmth on his face. 'So why is your father so protective of you?'

'My mother ran off, leaving him some years ago.'

'Oh, that had to be a hard thing to deal with.'

'I can't say that I blame her, my pa makes it near impossible to put up with him,' Alma said calmly.

'Then why do you and your brothers stay with your father?' Latimer asked simply.

'I don't have a choice, and as for my brothers, they are just like him.'

'And that's like what?'

'Overly protective, ill-mannered, ignorant, short-tempered, violent, and some of the meanest people I've ever seen,' she said without a hint of hyperbole.

Morgan Latimer smiled at her. 'Anything good about them?'

'They mean well. They were raised that way; my father brought them up to be just like him. But they're bigger than my pa.'

'How about you? You anything like them?'

'I'm a lady.'

'So I've noticed.'

Alma flushed with delight. 'Do you think I'm attractive?'

'That goes without saying,' Latimer said, nearly muttering.

Purposely, she allowed the blanket to fall off her shoulder, revealing the top of one smooth breast. Latimer looked, cleared his throat loudly, and then looked away. It wasn't that he didn't like women — his past experiences proved that wrong. There were some he liked a hell of a lot. It was just that, as a whole, he found women led to trouble. And trouble was what he was trying so hard to avoid. Trouble that he didn't need.

'Well, do you, Latimer?' Alma persisted. 'Think I'm attractive, that is?'

'I'm going to check on your clothes to make sure that they are drying properly,' he said, getting up in a hurry and walking off to check the clothes that he had hung over some sticks close enough to the fire to dry them out but not burn them. 'Yep, they're about done. Now, will you be OK in finding your way back home?'

'I don't know, those clothes still seem wet to me.' Alma Duke was on her feet. She was close to him now, her hand passed him slowly as she touched her skirt, a strand of her hair brushed against his face. Morgan Latimer consciously breathed out so as not to take in any more of her womanly fragrance than necessary.

Now she was leaning against his shoulder and felt soft enough to make a man forget whom he was and what he was doing. He looked up at her and she looked down. Their eyes met. Her smile was intoxicating, with just a hint of danger to it. As she made a move, she seemed to trip and predictably fell against his tall frame. He put his arm around her waist to steady her and the blanket fell open. Latimer found himself staring at a fully rounded, coral-nippled breast at especially close proximity and at that same instant a voice was heard that was the harshest, roughest sounding voice he had ever heard, filled the Texas countryside.

'What in the hell is goin' on *here*?'

The two of them spun around ashamedly.

Like the storm earlier, out of nowhere the campsite was filled with Duke men.

And just like the storm earlier, his world went dark.

6

This was precisely the sort of thing that Morgan Latimer meant about himself and trouble; he never went looking for it, but it always found him as unerringly as geese found their way south at the first sign of frost.

He had actually been nodding off by his peaceful little campfire in the nice warm cavern when the sounds of splashing and raised voices had drawn him down to the creek.

The sky was completely dark when Latimer returned again to consciousness. He possessed the appetite of the open, of the normal man in perfect physical health.

Two men stood together near the door to the room — one lean, dark-skinned, with a black goatee, the other heavily set with a closely trimmed gray beard. Morgan Latimer knew who they were, the Duke men, Alma's family. One of them was leaning against the door, one hand on his hip.

Here he was in the Dukes' sprawling communal home, nursing a whole flock of bruises and contusions, under the eye of a bunch of lying hill men and the sheriff of El Paso. He was missing a few hours, he surmised, from the time the Dukes had entered his camp until now. Holding onto his temper was making Morgan Latimer uncomfortable.

The Dukes also showed signs of rough usage. His memory was coming back to him. The big ruckus at the cavern had broken out when the hill family men had accused Latimer of interfering with their sister, then had announced their intention of hauling him up before the law. That was when Latimer had lost his temper and socked the big one called Grant so hard that he still couldn't see straight. But in the long term, it had proven a case of too many Dukes.

Then Morgan Latimer understood,

his heart beating rapidly, his teeth clenched to keep back an outburst of passion. So that was their game, was it? Some act of his had awakened the cowardly suspicions of those watching him.

Now Latimer had no option but to sit back and listen to them blacken his name to a lawman.

That was until a diversion in the shape of a cocky young man in a bright blue shirt arrived. He was chuckling, as though he found the situation too funny for words.

The young man was a Filmore, who were the Dukes' bitter foes. To a man, the Dukes fell ominously silent as Theo Filmore dropped into a chair, snapped his suspenders and smiled amiably. No Filmore would dare show his face around El Paso alone normally, but Theo felt he was safe enough with the law present.

'Don't pay me no mind, Sheriff,' Theo said cheerfully. 'But I just had to dog you out here when I heard why they'd sent for you. I want to be sure I've got the story straight when I go home to tell the family.' He looked quizzically at Morgan Latimer, seated in a corner. 'Is this here the feller that got his hands on Alma's delicates?'

'I did nothing of the sort!' Latimer snapped, but his words were ignored or not heard by those in attendance.

Obadiah Duke emitted a cry of outrage and frustration and launched himself at Theo Filmore like a big pine log shooting over a spillway. The solid chair that collapsed under their combined weight caused an explosive sound as the two men tumbled into a corner, and when a chair leg rolled Obadiah's way, he grabbed it and tried to batter Filmore's brains out with it.

But the Filmores were fighters and Theo was one of the best. Parrying the chair leg, he managed to get himself up out of the corner and uppercut big Obadiah so hard that he somersaulted backwards just as the sheriff was rushing in to stop the fight. The result was that the two men went down in a tangle of arms and legs, leaving Theo Filmore free to look for another target. Instead, Theo became the target.

The youngest Duke boy, Levi, caught him from behind with a quick jab that sent him lurching forward straight into Clayton, who punched him on the left ear, rapidly followed by Grant, who walloped him on the right ear.

Stunned and near deaf, Theo tripped over the sheriff and fell through the front door onto the porch, where he was easy picking for Clifton Duke, who kicked him into the yard expertly.

Throughout the uproar, Morgan Latimer sat back in the corner, wrapped in a cloak of revulsion and anger: revulsion at the violence and anger because of the fact that all these men were plainly hungry for trouble, while he only wanted peace. Yet he was the man with the deepest trouble of all.

The sheriff came back inside after seeing Filmore off, dabbing pensively at a cut lip. Obadiah Duke was nursing a nose bleed and cursing under his breath, while Grant and Clayton assured each other how much they would have enjoyed putting a bullet or two in Theo Filmore, had the law not been around at the time of his intrusion.

Alma Duke, seemingly immune to all the uproar, was watching the scowling Morgan Latimer with stars in her eyes.

The look might well have sent tremors of fear and uncertainty coursing through Latimer had he been more aware of the fact. Then again, he was oblivious. He was busy evaluating his position and contemplating whether he should try to make a break for it.

He realized the Dukes were beyond the pale. He had never seen anything like them outside the back hills of Kentucky. They were as wild and mean as a pack of Apaches or other Indians. They smelled awful and carried rifles as though they were extensions of their arms. He'd done nothing but rescue their sister from a fate worse than death, yet they insisted on treating him like a mad dog rapist. He would be lucky to get out of this alive — if he didn't make a break.

At the moment there was nobody between him and the back door, which somebody had carelessly left open.

Morgan Latimer bunched his long legs ready to spring into action.

Something round, cold and hard pressed against his neck just below his ear. The ugly face of Clifton Duke stared down at him along with the barrel of a rifle.

'I wouldn't iffen I were you, stranger!'

'Mr Duke, put down that rifle!' the sheriff barked halfheartedly.

'Then you git to it and do yer job, the one I'm payin' ye fer,' Duke countered. 'This here scoundrel was 'bout to make a run fer the back door.' He gave Latimer a final poke with the rifle barrel. 'Wasn't ye?'

Scoundrel?

This was the first time he had been

called that, he had been called many things, mind you . . . but he could not recall being labeled a scoundrel.

'Godforsaken, this here scoundrel was tryin' to disgrace my only sister,' remarked Grant. 'He's a bit thin, doesn't seem so tough, but iffen he wants to marry her . . . then . . .'

'I'm not marrying anyone!' Latimer exploded, coming to his feet in an instant. He glared at each of the Dukes in turn. 'I'm no scoundrel and I'm certainly no rapist!'

'I reckon the man's right,' weighed in the sheriff. He scratched his head, removing his hat first and then said, 'I've got this here fella down as a potential rapist, for assault, assault with a deadly weapon, assault on a woman, foul language, disorderly conduct, resisting arrest and anything else I can think of . . . but I don't think he carried out the act of raping . . . so he can't be charged with that.'

'Incredible!' Latimer said. 'You don't know a damn thing, you're all insane! I didn't do anything to that girl!'

'Well, iffen we hadn't arrived in time, he sure woulda raped poor Alma there,' Clifton Duke said in an ominous tone. 'It was a good thing we showed up when we did . . . this fella may have killed poor Alma once he'd done his business.'

'Right!' Grant Duke stood straddle-legged in the center of the office with his rifle angled at Latimer. The mean expression in his eyes indicated that in about forty years' time he would be a dead ringer for his father if he were to grow a beard, shrink about eight or nine inches and lose a hundred or more pounds. 'We knew this fella was up to no good as soon as we laid eyes upon him. He was goin' to harm poor Alma, my sister, Sheriff. It's the code of the hills, he's spoiled her, so he could marry her.'

'Nah, I don't want to see this scoundrel with Alma,' young Levi put in, toying with his rifle. 'Like, he don't have to marry her, do he?'

'No, he don't,' Clifton Duke agreed. 'He could hang for his crimes.'

Morgan Latimer couldn't believe this was happening. It had to be some kind of bad joke or worse — a nightmare. This wasn't the dark ages. This was Texas, 1869. He turned desperately to the sheriff, who suddenly began to appear like a blade of grass wavering with the wind. It was obvious the man had no backbone.

'You can't allow this! This is against the law!' Latimer almost shouted.

'Well,' the sheriff sighed, 'we probably should have a proper trial and all.'

'A trial for what? I didn't do anything against the law!' Morgan Latimer was now shouting. 'Ask the girl.'

'She clearly isn't in her right mind,' Clifton Duke said as his daughter blushed demurely and dropped her eyes. 'Besides, it's done already.' He lifted his rifle. 'What's it gonna be, stranger? Marriage or the rope?'

Morgan Latimer said a word that should have made Alma blush an even

71

deeper shade of red, but it didn't. Some choice! And yet, casting a quick, reluctant glance over to Alma's lush curves, he sensed it was one he'd already made. It would be better to lie in her arms tonight than in a grave.

Morgan Latimer groaned. The choice they were offering was no choice at all. As though the words had aroused him from a bad dream, he turned to front the stern, bearded face of Clifton Duke.

The mean old man interpreted his groan as agreement. 'Fine,' he said with a look of disappointment. 'Clayton, go and fetch the reverend. Sheriff, you'll be our witness. There's goin' to be a weddin', and let's see that it's fairly done.'

Morgan Latimer groaned again.

7

The quiet that had fallen over the Filmore place wasn't natural. They were an exuberant family, the Filmores of the Golden Plume ranch, and there was usually a lot of talk, roughhousing, fiddle playing or other music and/or hard work being done about the place. But when Narcissa Filmore, her sons Theo and Garrett, her daughters Lena and Tara, and any other members of the family: cousins, uncles, friends who might as well be blood related, were all wearing brooding looks and not saying much at all, it usually meant one of two things: somebody had died, or they were hatching a plan.

No Filmore had died in some time, since Uncle Seth had gone out in a failed bank robbery in Waco after losing his life's savings in a card game the night before.

That meant something was brewing . . .

The girls knew it, but weren't interested. Lena and Tara were as pretty as pictures and prettier than any women this side of the Rio Grande, however, neither had shown any proclivity of being interested in the feud over the years, despite the best efforts of their mother to get them involved.

Lena and Tara were interested in only one thing — boys. Well, mostly boys; at times they did show an interest in dancing, visiting the town, pretty dresses, fast horses and swimming naked in Willow Creek on hot summer days and evenings. They obediently attended the numerous funerals, and were usually on hand to nurse brothers, cousins, uncles, and friends following the frequent outbreaks of violence that had made the name of El Paso County notorious across the West, and occasionally they were heard to direct the odd required expletive towards the Dukes. But they didn't really mean it, and everyone knew it. In this regard, they were a severe regret to their mother.

Narcissa Filmore's revulsion almost compensated for her daughters' lack of it. Still attractive in a cold-eyed way, she was Clifton Duke's foil from the opposite end of the trouble-torn area, and was every bit as intimidating an adversary as that old back shooter, Clifton Duke. When Narcissa Filmore hated, she gave it all she had, and in this was skillfully held by Garrett and Theo.

The twin male Filmores were the best-looking men in the area, tall and put together well with clear, green eyes and bright smiles that charmed the girls of the El Paso area and made everyone named Duke sick to their stomachs. Garrett and Theo could shoot, ride, raise hell, chase the ladies, and fight with the best of them, but the thing they did the best was animosity towards the Dukes.

It didn't take much to bring on an

attack of the Dukes' hatred, and the beating Theo had taken in town earlier in the day had proven more than spur enough. Of course, some might contend that Theo had had no business challenging the nemesis in their lair but he had been overcome by inquisitiveness to investigate the reports he'd heard about Alma and the drifter, and had considered his incursion into town worth the risk.

The sheriff's presence in El Paso and Willow Glen hadn't been enough to defend him from taking a good licking however, and he now sported several bruises and gashes as evidence of what a thorough job the Dukes had done to him.

This had made Garrett angry, and he badly wanted to square the matter. But this wasn't the reason why Garrett, his brother, his mother, and a clutch of friends and cousins were encircled in brooding silence at McKelligon Canyon as the moonlit glen night wore on.

They were thinking about weddings,

and how hill weddings weren't any different from the usual kind, insofar as they always brought a slew of people together at a time when they weren't as vigilant as they usually might have been.

If your name was either Duke or Filmore, you lived in a constant stage of vigilance here; otherwise there was a decent chance you wouldn't live long at all. It was unusual indeed that one side let down its guard, but Narcissa Filmore believed tonight might be such an occasion, and she was usually right about such matters.

Garrett Filmore broke a long silence when he said, 'Somethin' just struck me . . . ' He raised an eyebrow at his twin. 'What did this drifter look like again?'

'Tall feller,' supplied Theo, tenderly touching a swollen lip, courtesy of a Clifton Duke kick. 'Lean and stringy . . . with broad shoulders.'

'Uh huh.' Garrett shook his head. 'And you said he didn't miss one of the

Dukes in the fight they had with him down along the Willow.'

'That's *keyrect*.' Theo frowned as he tested his teeth for looseness. 'What are you gettin' at?'

'Clear as day,' Theo said, squinting at his mother, who sat agonizing at the table. 'He's a tough one. The Dukes ain't just gainin' a son-in-law, but another rifle.'

Narcissa looked up severely. She hadn't considered this facet of the pending shotgun nuptials between Morgan Latimer and Alma Duke. But it was cousin Jasper Hammond, a smallish version of Theo and Garrett who spoke up. 'I dunno what you're gettin' so worked up about,' he said. 'This shotgun weddin' won't come off. Alma won't go through with it.'

Everyone gaped at him, bewildered by his confident tone. They were about to question him, when a hand came into the ranch house to advise that a visitor was on his way in from the gate. Russell Denson had come a calling.

'He's got word of what's happening here in the glen with the Dukes,' prophesied Narcissa Filmore, getting to her feet. A deep scowl creased her forehead. She was a lovely woman, even though her face was lined with bitterness. All the Filmores were comely, a fact which didn't endear them to the homely Dukes. 'Wonder what he wants here.'

'Whatever it is, Mother,' pronounced Tara, idly brushing her glossy red hair before a gilt mirror, 'you can bet it will cause more trouble.'

'Every cent you've got,' affirmed Lena, who was draped stylishly over a big leather couch, admiring her ankles. She shuddered. 'He creeps me out.'

One of the small problems in Russell Denson's life was that nobody liked him, and that went double for the prettier girls of the glen whom he was regularly attempting to interest in his far from interesting self. But despite his shortage of physical charm, Denson was no man to be taken lightly. It was well known that he was the area's wealthiest citizen, but it wasn't generally known how much power he wielded, nor just how far and high his ambitions stretched. Not everyone knew that Denson followed a policy of pouring lamp oil on the flames of the volatile Duke-Filmore feud.

It was this that brought him to the rambling homestead in McKelligon Canyon that night.

8

The El Paso lock-up was an improvised affair, although it didn't seem to be used much. It was originally a two-room cabin with gable to the street, the front apartment at one time a low groggery, the keeper sleeping in the rear room. Whether sudden death, or financial reverses, had been the cause, the community had in some manner become possessed of the property, and had at once dedicated it to the commonweal. For the purpose thus selected it was rather well adapted, being strongly built, easily guarded, and on the outskirts of the town. With iron grating over the windows, the back door heavily spiked, and the front secured by iron bars, any prisoner once locked within could probably be found when wanted.

He was alone, with only the faintest

murmur of voices coming to him through the thick partition. It was a room some twelve feet square; open to the roof, with bare walls, and containing no furniture except a rude bench. Still dazed by the suddenness of his situation, he sank down upon the seat, leaned his head on his hands, and endeavored to think. It was difficult to get the facts marshalled into any order or to comprehend clearly the situation, yet little by little his brain grasped the main details, and he awoke to a full realization of his condition, of the forces he must war against.

His choices: die or marry.

Morgan Latimer was essentially a man of action, a fighter by instinct, and so long accustomed to danger that the excitement of it merely put new fire into his veins. Now that he understood exactly what threatened, all numbing feeling of hesitancy and doubt vanished, and he became instantly alive. He would not lie there in that hole waiting for the formation of a mob of angry men who had the wrong impression of what had transpired on the creek's banks; nor would he trust in things working out in his favor.

Experience told him otherwise.

He lifted his head, every nerve tingling with desperate determination. The low growl of voices was audible through the partition, but there was no other sound. El Paso was still resting, and there would be neither crowd nor excitement until much later, he thought, attending his sudden wedding.

He ran his eyes about the room, searching for some spot of weakness. It was dark back of the bench, and he turned in that direction. He was going to make an attempt to escape.

'Don't bother,' someone said. 'You ain't gettin' out of marryin' my sister,' Obadiah Duke said from the darkened doorway.

'Look,' Latimer started to say.

'Save it, drifter,' Obadiah replied. 'Now, c'mon, time for you to get hitched.'

★ ★ ★

Candlelight gleamed softly on the bride's improvised wedding gown and upon the ruddy features of the Reverend Uriah Redden. It tinted the weathered, big-nosed faces of an assortment of Dukes, and revealed how pale the tall bridegroom's face was as he stood staring straight ahead, looking more like a man attending a funeral than his own wedding.

The gentle light tinted the leather binding of the Bible in the minister's none too steady hands, highlighted a happy tear on Alma's pink cheek, and put a nice soft sheen down the barrel of the shotgun in Clifton Duke's gnarled old hands as he growled, 'Git a move on with this thing!'

The preacher swallowed. This really wasn't his kind of wedding. If he had had his druthers, he would rather have officiated at a marriage ceremony where everyone, particularly the bride and groom, turned up voluntarily. He felt it made for a far happier and even spiritual atmosphere. Still, these were the Mesa Hills, and it was a Duke affair, which meant that one could not necessarily rely upon things being done according to the book.

'Ahem!' the Reverend Redden cleared his throat as he glanced around the large room. 'Is everyone present?'

A good question . . . apart from a collection of assorted Dukes and the sheriff, who looked hot and bothered in the candlelight, there was nobody else in attendance: no neighbors and no friends from town.

The explanation for this was simple. Due to the fact that years of violent feuding with the Filmores had driven other settlers from the Mesa Hills in droves, the Dukes didn't have any close neighbors to invite in to see their daughter, sister or cousin tie the knot. As for town folk . . . well, the Dukes could take them or leave them. What they were looking for tonight was a quick, legal, no-nonsense wedding — not some showy affair with everyone getting drunk and making speeches. They wanted Alma hitched up and honor satisfied, and you didn't need herds of people to do that.

Clifton Duke spoke from the other corner of his mouth in an almost hateful tone, 'We don't have all the time in the world, preacher!'

'Is that so?' the Reverend Uriah Redden of the Revival Christian Church muttered. He was pretty sauced on rye whiskey as he was every night. 'I was just reflecting how sad it is that the good Mrs Duke could not attend to see her only daughter marry.'

A hush was over the room.

Every eye went to Clifton Duke as always happened whenever his long departed wife was brought up in conversation. Duke had never forgiven his wife for walking out on him many years ago, although accounts of what had brought about the rift were countless and varied. The truth wasn't pretty. It had to do with the birth of the Duke's youngest, Levi. It had been a difficult delivery, and afterwards, while the mother was lying spent, only moderately proud of having brought yet another Duke into the world, her husband had announced that on this joyous occasion, he was insisting on choosing the baby's name. They would call him Duke. Duke Duke.

Following an exhausting argument, during which Mrs Duke rallied long enough to smash her husband to the floor with a large vase, it was agreed that Levi would be a more appropriate name. Nevertheless, the mother never recovered from the incident, and when the first opportunity presented itself, she took flight for parts unknown, leaving her ugly husband and his four, mean-spirited sons and daughter to fend for themselves.

The shotgun left Morgan Latimer's rigid back and pointed at the man holding the good book. Clifton Duke's face looked pitted and scarred as though from smallpox.

Glancing from the shotgun to that face, the nervous preacher got on with the ceremony, sweating more profusely than before.

'My dear beloved, on this solemn occasion that sees us gathered here tonight . . . '

'No one died . . . yet. This here's a weddin',' Grant Duke hissed, and Redden was quickly back on the tracks.

' . . . gathered here tonight on this truly joyous occasion . . . '

As his voice droned on, the Dukes, all armed, kept their eyes on the bridegroom. They were ready to shoot if he tried any tricks.

'Go through with it like a man and everythin' will be fine,' Clifton Duke had counseled. 'But iffen you so much as blink when you ain't supposed to, you'll never get married to our Alma or anyone else for that fact.'

Apart from the father, who stood directly behind the happy couple with his double barreled shotgun, the bride-to-be's brothers were drawn up in a line leading from the oldest down to the youngest.

Obadiah stood at Grant's shoulder, a hulking giant with almost invisible eyes and a well-deserved reputation for having never been known to put his great strength to any worthwhile use.

Clayton was the sharp one. Shorter, leaner and faster than Grant and Obadiah, he was a foul-tempered runt who had shot more people than anyone else in the clan, apart from his father.

Levi was little more than a kid, but already all the vicious Duke character-istics were well entrenched in his makeup, and he was getting to be a real expert with a hunting knife.

The collection of cousins who formed a half-circle behind the immediate family all had the undeni-able Duke look about them, although none was anywhere near the size of Grant or Obadiah, and happily, none were quite as reptilian-looking as their father. They were enjoying the ceremony; they planned to get as drunk as humanly possible afterwards.

'I love weddings,' Redden interrupted the ceremony to remark.

Clifton Duke scowled ferociously and hissed, 'Git on with it, you damned fool! It's taking so long it may well turn into a funeral.'

Although he stood staring at a spot a foot above the primed-up preacher's head, and had done so ever since being brought into the room where he was to meet his doom, Morgan Latimer knew exactly where each Duke was and precisely what he was doing at any given moment.

His legs tingled and his feet itched inside his boots. The Latimer body wanted to run, but the Latimer brain said, 'Don't try it!' They were watching him. They expected him to try to bolt. He wouldn't get two yards. The sons of bitches!

A light film of perspiration shone on Latimer's weathered features as he half-listened to the drunken preacher drone on. With every minute, he could feel the shackles tightening. Soon, he would be a married man. A husband! Him, who had never wanted to be anything but free — to go where he wanted; to do what he wanted, and all because he'd gone to the aid of a maiden in distress.

He glanced sideways at the maiden, who flashed him an encouraging, morale-boosting smile with two rows of healthy, milk-white, country-girl teeth. At least, he brooded, one of them seemed to be enjoying it all.

'I think we should now pause and perhaps sing a hymn or two . . . ' suggested Uriah Redden, but got no farther as Clifton Duke cut in on him.

'We'll all sing like goddamn nightingales,' Clifton Duke said irreverently. 'Afterwards. Git it — '

'I know,' the reverend said with just a trace of irritation. 'Git . . . I mean get it done. Very well then, where was I?'

He was up to the part about

honoring and treasuring. He liked this segment of the ceremony best and raised his voice. The sonorous tones carried beyond the big room, drifted across the yard, where the Dukes' horses dozed at hitching posts, were moving within shadows and starlight glinted and winked silently on the barrels of pistols, rifles, shotguns and one repeating carbine.

The repeating carbine was the property of Garrett Filmore, who used the weapon as a bar to hold back the largest horse the Dukes owned as the big roan eagerly tried to push beyond the barn shadows into the yard itself.

'Steady,' Garrett cautioned, watching the house. 'Just because we don't see any sentries don't mean for sure there ain't none.'

Everyone halted to survey the scene. There were nine in the bunch, each man at least partially primed on good moonshine, each committed to the age-old feudist's principle of getting square. Between them, the Filmores and their kinfolk had enough grievances against the Dukes to fuel a full-scale war. The Dukes, of course, came at least as well equipped with a catalogue of hatreds against them, and there were protagonists on either side who believed the slate could never be wiped clean until the last of the enemy was dead and buried.

When blood feuds such as this caught hold, the first casualty was usually common sense.

The smell of rot-gut whiskey was strong in the air as the Filmores watched and listened. They had needed the powerful liquor to get them going tonight, to take advantage of the enemy's preoccupation with the wedding. The theory was that the Dukes would be so intent on what was happening behind their lamp-lit windows, they wouldn't realize the danger they were in until it was too late.

It seemed a good enough theory, but had still needed the liquid courage of some foul smelling whiskey. They had

Denson to thank for supplying them with both the booze and motivation. They would be in his debt — if they didn't get killed.

Theo Filmore said softly, 'We can't wait any longer, Garrett. It'll all be over soon.'

'I still don't know why Alma's goin' through with this,' complained cousin Jasper Hammond, but fell silent as everyone hushed him.

'All right,' Garrett replied with one final glance around at the others. 'Just remember, when we hit, we hit 'em hard. We ain't takin' no prisoners tonight.'

'Let's go,' Theo said. 'You boys first.'

As the 'soldiers' moved out across the starlit yard, the 'generals', Theo and Garrett glanced at each other. The twins were close. Apart from the feuding that marred their lives, they were high-spirited, fun-loving, life-appreciating young men who loved the Western lifestyle and loved to have a good time. But each understood only too well what was involved here tonight. This was to be no skirmish. This would be a major assault right at the enemy's heart. A man could be killed.

They silently shook hands and followed the others across the yard just as Levi Duke's dog succeeded in climbing from a nail keg to an egg crate, then to a carpenter's horse, and from there, reached the workbench of the tack room adjacent to the meat house.

Because Clifton Duke hated dogs in general, along with just about everything else, and this dog in particular, he'd ordered the animal locked up during the ceremony in case it should intrude on the 'dignity' of the occasion. The dog was still well and truly locked away, but when it reached the tack room window to see a group of stealthy figures moving across the yard towards the house, it immediately set up a racket that went through the house like a dozen alarm bells ringing simultaneously just as the parson was trying to coerce a tight-lipped Morgan Latimer into saying his 'I do'.

The hysterical barking galvanized every Duke into action, and as they whipped out their guns and charged towards the front windows, Latimer muttered, 'No, the hell I don't,' under his breath and legged it for the rear of the house.

Alma Duke screamed as the first shot rang out.

It was all she could do.

9

The dive that took Morgan Latimer through the window carried him across the dimly lit back porch in a shower of glass. He landed on one shoulder, narrowly missing an upright. As he skidded off the porch into the dust, the deep-throated roar of warring weapons crashed around the compound atop the Duke complex, and somewhere, a man howled as if he had been hit.

Latimer sprang to his feet and shot a glance over his shoulder in time to see one of the Duke cousins aiming a six gun at him.

As he ducked low, the .44 went off and the slug whistled over the curve of his back and slammed into the side of a buckboard wagon parked behind him.

Morgan Latimer ran towards the shadows of the tank stand, his long legs covering the ground in giant bounds as the .44 snarled again and he heard the bullet sizzle through the air.

Behind him, the lights were now going out in the house as the defenders, realizing the seriousness of the attack, took every precaution.

By now, there were wounded men on either side and the bellowing crescendo of the six shooters was growing even louder as Latimer reached his objective then halted, looking for a way across the open space of the yard.

It didn't look good. Gun-toting figures were blasting their way around the flanks of the big old house now, some heading towards his position. Once he quit the tank stand he would be clearly visible to gunmen on either side.

What he needed was a gun of his own. He needed his gun, his Winchester rifle.

He waited maybe half a minute or so before an attacker came scuttling towards him with shots from the darkened windows, lifting geysers of earth behind his flying feet. As the running man came charging into the shadows, Morgan Latimer let fly with a swinging fist that sent him cartwheeling in one direction with his Colt spinning in the other.

Latimer plucked the weapon neatly from the air, ducked low as a ricochet came whizzing by, and was about to make a break for it when he saw a vaguely familiar face over by the corner of the house.

He realized it was the man who had come to the house earlier to get a good working over by the Dukes — Theo Filmore.

So, it was the feud in full force! He should have surmised. Not that he was about to complain. Maybe they'd saved him from a fate worse than death, although whether they had saved him from death itself remained to be seen.

'Fall back!' Theo Filmore suddenly shouted as a man close to him went down, clutching a shattered leg. 'There's too many of the bastards and we don't have the surprise on our side any longer.'

'You can say that again,' Latimer noted. The Dukes were really stepping up their fire now, and there was a lot of yelling going on within the house.

With guns spewing hot and red from all compass points, Latimer launched himself from cover and went streaking for the wagon shed. He was zigzagging violently as bullets began zipping around him. He sensed the shots were coming from the house, but didn't have either the time or the interest to confirm this.

The wagon shed loomed closer. He covered the final yards in a headlong dive that carried him into the doorway, rolling himself into a ball as the blackness engulfed him, then kicking off to one side to get out of the firing line.

Latimer lay full length with his hands supporting him for a handful of seconds, sucking air into his laboring lungs. Then, without even pausing for an ironical thought about how much trouble peace-loving Morgan Latimer had managed to land himself in yet again, he lunged erect and trotted off through the gloomy building to reach a side door that gave onto a section of the yard bordered on three sides by the wagon shed, the gate and a bunkhouse. The fourth side was open, giving into the main yard, where the feud still raged on even though the attackers were now in full retreat.

He had to get himself a horse.

As he quit the shed, a hidden rifleman began shooting at him from the shadowed area between the bunkhouse and the tack room. Latimer lifted the Colt and fired two shots towards the gun flash. He didn't want to kill anyone here tonight, but certainly wouldn't apologize if he did. As far as he could assess, there wasn't a hair's-breadth between the factions when it came to lunacy, although he supposed, for obvious reasons, his sympathies would favor the Filmores at this point.

The sniper quit shooting for a moment, enabling Latimer to gain the bunkhouse. Jerking open the door, he ran through the darkened building to reach a window that gave onto a tree-lined yard, where he made out the silhouettes of men rushing for their horses in the tree shadows.

Nobody even challenged the long, lean figure that suddenly bobbed up and vaulted into an empty saddle; the others were too busy getting themselves away as rifle fire from the house continued to sweep the broad yards clear.

Crouched low over the horse's neck, Latimer used his heels to drive the animal into a dead gallop as he went careering away through the timber which fringed the Dukes' ranch like the hair on a monk's head.

Avoiding the other riders, he set himself a downhill course towards Mission Valley. Long before he reached his destination, the fierce shooting faded then died away altogether.

Up at the Dukes' ranch, it was time to take stock, and the disappearance of Alma's perspective groom seemed the least of their troubles. Seven men had been wounded in the fray, while Cousin Elmer Duke from over the Texas way was eventually found lying on the broad of his back, out by the pump, staring wide-eyed at the stars but not seeing any of them.

10

Midmorning the next day found El Paso very jittery despite the fact that the feud barely touched the town itself.

Blood had been spilled at the Duke compound and a man had lost his life. That was more than enough to set the town on edge, and the tension was thick enough to cut with a knife when a man on the gallery of the hotel looked towards the eastern trail and announced, 'Stranger headin' this a way!'

The townsfolk paused in what they were doing at that moment to stare. The lone rider was coming in off a bridge; a tall, rangy man astride a brown gelding. They didn't recognize the rider, but the liveryman was quick to identify the horse belonging to a man called Giant, a staunch Filmore friend, strongly suspected of having taken part in the shootout at the Duke ranch overnight.

'Somebody better tell that to the horse,' a mustached cowboy said, but his companions disagreed. 'It belongs to the Giant.'

'He'll find out soon enough. We don't want to kick the hornet's nest any more than it has been all ready, do we?' another man said plainly.

They certainly did not. El Paso was a formerly prosperous town, which had started to see a decline of late, mainly due to the feud. Over the years, the valley's smaller settlers had been driven out one by one by the violence, and once gone, were not replaced. New homesteaders looking for a place to settle down and raise cattle, crops and kids, shied away from the Mesa Hills on hearing about the feud and seeing the outsized graveyard.

Business was in decline too, and doubtless would suffer even more as word of last night's bloodbath spread to neighboring towns. What El Paso definitely did not need more of today, was trouble. It had had enough. But whether trouble had had enough of El Paso was open to conjecture. The lone rider coming in from the bridge was a man who knew a great deal about trouble's caprices, even more in fact than he had known the day he'd first seen the welcoming dusty outline of the Mesa Hills.

Conversation dried up as the horseman rounded the corner of the boarded up El Paso General Goods Store. They saw that, as well as being taller and bigger than most, wide of hip and broad of shoulder, he had a long-boned face composed of taut planes and angles, a hard jaw set like a chunk of granite, and a pair of flinty hazel eyes that seemed to register disapproval of everything he saw in El Paso's sunny morning.

The townsfolk looked at the way the stranger wore his gun, then looked at each other.

'Hey, you don't reckon it's another

one of them, do ya?'

The man who spoke was an unemployed blacksmith, and he directed his question to an unemployed saddler. One thing El Paso wasn't short of was men out of work. The feud that was driving honest people out of the Mesa Hills and deterring others from coming to town was bleeding business dry. There was a number of able-bodied men around town who had nothing better to do than sit about and gossip.

'One of what?' muttered the saddler.

'One of them there gunslingers.'

Everyone remembered when the Filmores had hired themselves a two-gun ranny from the border to bolster their clan's performance in the feud. It had been a disaster. The gunslinger, slick and mean, had seemed unable to differentiate between Dukes and Filmores, and ended up winging several from both factions before the clans briefly joined forces to tar and feather him and run him out of town on a greased rail. Since that turbulent experience, the two sides had sought support only amongst family and friends.

'He ain't no gunslinger,' the cowboy said with conviction. 'Look at his rig. He's nothing but a drifter.'

'Big lookin' drifter,' corrected the liveryman. 'Looks mean enough to scare a rattlesnake, don't he?'

'Big and lean, like a wolf,' added another man.

That was putting it mildly. Morgan Latimer was even madder than that. In the space of some sixteen hours he had been set up by rifle-toting hillbillies, beaten up, accused of many and varied crimes, humiliated, called horrendous names, forced to front up for a shotgun wedding and subsequently shot at repeatedly, with intent to do serious bodily harm, by an assortment of men he didn't even know. He had misplaced his own horse and spent the night trying to sleep in a leaky cave while keeping one eye open for further trouble.

Mad?

Mad wasn't the word to describe what he was. He was infuriated.

The horse's hoofs raised little puffs of dust as the rider traveled down the center of the street with the climbing sun throwing his shadow before him.

Latimer's slit eyes cut left and right. This was his first look at El Paso and he wasn't overly impressed. It seemed that every second or third business was shuttered up. It was a sizeable town with enormous potential he could see, yet seemed short of citizens and life.

The sudden lifting of the breeze drew his attention to a long calico sign slung across the street between the hotel and the town hall. In colored letters a foot high, the sign read:

ANNUAL WAGON RACES
$500 PRIZE MONEY!

Latimer's top lip turned into a sneer. A wagon race? In fine print, it read that there were different categories: covered wagon, Conestoga wagon, and surreys (with and without a fringe). Seemed to him they had been better off using the $500 in prize money to employ vermin exterminators to rid the place of various Dukes, Filmores, and others of their ilk. That's what he would do if he was in charge, which, luckily, he was not.

There was no sign of his strawberry roan.

He slowed the horse he rode when he saw a saloon, which advertised:

WHISKEY! FARO! GIRLS!

Faro and girls he could do without at the moment, but the thought of a big, smooth, double shot of bourbon or something close to it aroused his taste buds like so many grizzlies awakening from hibernation.

But as he turned the horse towards the saloon, he sighted the badge.

Bourbon suddenly became secondary and instead, Morgan Latimer swung his horse across to the jailhouse and reined in before the lawman who was standing on his top step, sunning himself.

For a moment, Sheriff Abel Stark wasn't aware of him. He was a very preoccupied peace officer that morning, having been a reluctant witness and participant in one of the most violent outbreaks of the Duke-Filmore feud in a long time.

The sheriff had taken a bullet burn to his thigh, and in the chilly light of dawn several hours earlier, had had the onerous task of informing Elmer Duke's family of his untimely and unfortunate death. He was a man weighted down by many grave concerns. And when he finally looked up to see Morgan Latimer sitting his saddle staring at him through cold eyes, it certainly didn't cheer him up any.

'You!' The sheriff was startled. 'What are you doing here?'

Morgan Latimer exhaled and paused before answering.

'Is there any reason I shouldn't be

here, Sheriff?' Latimer finally said in response.

'Every reason, man. If they see you again, it could start the whole thing off afresh.'

Latimer hooked a leg over the saddle pommel and pushed back his hat.

'By 'they', I take it you mean the Dukes?' he drawled.

'Damned right. They'll be in for the funeral later. I don't reckon it'd be a good idea for you to be here, Mr Latimer.'

'Oh, you don't, huh? So, what do you reckon I should do, Sheriff? Cut and run?' Latimer asked pretentiously.

'I'd recommend it strongly,' the sheriff replied.

'Go to hell.'

Sheriff Abel Stark blinked. 'What did you say to me?'

Latimer leapt down and loomed over the lawman, hands on hips, jaw outthrust, belligerence in every inch.

'I don't know what breed of lawman you are, Stark, but I'm startin' to get some idea. You saw what happened to me. You knew I only stepped in to help that girl last night, knew those bad-smellin' Dukes had no legal right to do what they did. Yet you just stood by and watched while they tried to hitch me up to Alma — and would have done if the Filmores hadn't shown up.' He paused to thump his chest with a hard forefinger. 'I'm the man that has been beat up, lost his horse, come close as dammit to getting shot a dozen times, all through no fault of my own, and you're tellin' me I should move on!'

'Now, calm yerself, Mr Latimer . . . '

'Easy? I've a hunch I could make a better sheriff out of a skunkweed. Have you seen my horse, a strawberry roan?'

'No, not yet. I — '

'Of course you haven't,' Latimer snapped, leading the mammoth horse off. 'That would be too much like doin' the job you're paid for, wouldn't it?'

Abel Stark opened his mouth to retort, but thought better of it. He needed to conserve his energy, he advised himself. He had a bad feeling that things were going to get even worse as a result of last night's flare-up.

He wished Morgan Latimer would go, but had an uncomfortable feeling he wouldn't.

The El Paso town diner advertised 'Good Hot Grub for the Working Man'. Latimer went inside, and the first customer he saw was the Reverend Uriah Redden, drinking his breakfast from a crockery cup. The preacher was obliged to hold the cup with both hands due to a bad case of the shakes. Last night, he'd spent one of the longest ten minutes of his life lying under a bed while the Duke house shook, rumbled and rattled to the roar of a full-blooded shootout. The preacher had prayed for deliverance, and his prayers had not gone unanswered. Whether or not he'd also prayed for Morgan Latimer was unknown, but like the sheriff, he appeared surprised to see him still around.

'Steak, potatoes and a cup of

whatever the Reverend is drinkin',' Morgan Latimer said to the man behind the counter.

'I'm pleased to see you survived the ruckus last night,' the Reverend Uriah Redden stated.

'I'm sure.'

'I'll bet that when you woke this morning, Mr Latimer, you were, um, relieved to say the least, to find yourself still single and unattached?'

Taking tobacco and papers from his shirt pocket, Latimer commenced rolling a cigarette. His cup of whiskey arrived and he took a sip then grimaced, wondering if his teeth had melted.

'Thrilled to bits,' he said.

'Do I detect certain hostility, Mr Latimer?' Reverend Redden asked.

'Me, hostile? Perish the thought, Reverend.'

Redden drained his cup, studied Latimer a moment longer, then slid off his stool. 'I must go and prepare for the funeral.'

'I see. I understand that in this town, marrying and burying can keep a man like you busy.'

Still looking unsure, the parson made his unsteady way out, leaving Latimer to attack his food, breaking off every now and then for a puff of his smoke and a sip of his whiskey. It might not have been everyone's idea of a healthy start to a day, but it was certainly setting him up.

'Seconds?' the man behind the counter asked.

'Nope, I'm good for now.'

The man nodded. 'Couldn't help but overhear. I guess you're the jasper the Dukes tried to railroad into marrying Alma, huh?'

'That would be me.'

'You ain't afraid they might try it again?'

The battle light flickered in Latimer's eyes. 'I'd sure like to see them try.'

The doors crashed open and a swaggering, hairy man wearing greasy buckskins breezed in and grabbed a

116

stool next to Latimer.

'A bucket of chili,' he growled before introducing himself. 'Jason Kirby. You're him — I mean, Latimer. Heard about last night. Crazy, huh? Hey, Jimmy, where's my Hell Paso coffee?'

Latimer eyed the newcomer warily as he was served with his cup of whiskey. But before he could speak, Kirby looked at him and said, 'Want a word of advice?'

'Leave town?'

'That'd be it.'

'I'm stayin'.'

Jason Kirby slapped the bar and laughed. 'Goddamn glad to hear it. You know, Latimer, I've seen so many so-called men pushed, kicked, squeezed and railroaded out of this man's town in my time that it does my old heart good to meet somebody with the grit and gumption to stay on, even though it'll likely get him killed. Yessir, I sure enough am.'

'Killed?'

'Well, man, the Dukes hate your guts,

and I hear you steamrolled a couple of Filmores last night, so I reckon it's a good bet that with that kind of reputation, you won't last long in Hell Paso, iffen you hang around too much longer.' He lifted his cup. 'Cheers.'

Latimer didn't drink. 'Why does everyone put up with it?'

'Because they don't want to end up dead.'

'Have you been threatened or shot at by them?'

'Once, maybe twice.'

'By who?'

'Does it matter? In this county when a man gets shot at, he dives for cover; he don't hang around tryin' to find out who did the shootin'.'

'That's ridiculous. You must all like it this way then.'

'Why?'

'On account as you are so cheerful.'

Jason Kirby slapped the counter again, grinning. 'Hell, that's only 'cause I'm gonna be $500 richer in a few days.'

'You're entering the racing contest?' Latimer asked.

'Key-rection . . . I'm going to win the racing contest. Best wagoner in the territory, that's Jason Kirby. Do you figure you'll be here to watch me win, Latimer?'

But Latimer wasn't listening; his eye had caught movement in the street outside. A Duke had just ridden into view on a high-shouldered strawberry roan. His strawberry roan!

Dumping some money on the bar, Latimer snatched up his hat and strode out, banging the green door. Obadiah Duke, sporting a black eye and with bandages around one thick leg, looked at the tall figure blankly for a moment before recognition set in. Then he reined in with a curse.

'Don't say it!' Latimer warned. 'Yeah, I'm still here. Now, get off that goddamned horse.'

Obadiah Duke was a big man, tall, broad and thick of muscle. He'd had a bad night, and rolled up in his saddlebag was a black coat he intended wearing to his cousin's funeral later in the day. His frame of mind was anything but rational or good, and the sight of Morgan Latimer bearing down on him with his mouth flapping a mile a minute did nothing to improve it.

Duke threw a leg over the pommel and dropped to the ground, wincing as his injured leg absorbed the shock.

'After what you done to my sister . . . ' he began, but Latimer didn't allow him to finish that sentence. Elbowing him roughly aside, he reached for the horse's reins.

Obadiah Duke cursed again and threw a punch, just as Latimer had hoped and expected he would.

The blow never landed. Morgan Latimer brushed it away with a fast left hand, then snapped his head forward to deliver a head butt to Obadiah's forehead. Passers-by heard the crunch of contact half a block away, and turned to see Obadiah Duke clutching at the saddle of Latimer's strawberry roan, trying to hold himself up on legs that had suddenly turned to mush. Latimer grinned right in the stunned man's face then calmly measured him off and knocked him off his feet with a haymaker composed of some muscle, some technique, and a whole lot of bad temper.

Obadiah Duke hit the street, all ironed out without a crease.

Latimer was beginning to feel better as he led the giant roan across to the hitch rail to transfer some of his gear from the borrowed horse. From the corner of his eye, he was aware of the sheriff watching him from his porch rocker, along with just about everybody else in the street.

'I'm a peace-lovin' man,' Latimer muttered to himself, 'but enough is enough.'

He didn't see the group of men emerge from the general store two doors down. The bunch had come out to see what the excitement was about, but the biggest of them, a man who looked like a grizzly bear standing on its hind legs, saw something unexpected. It was his own horse, missing since last night's affray at the Duke compound.

They called him the Giant, for very obvious reasons. And the boardwalk creaked beneath the Giant's weight as he made his way along to the diner's hitch rail to claim what was his.

Trouble was the Giant wasn't polite about it. He too, had had a bad night. The Filmore clan, of which he was a dues-paid member, had hoped to strike a death blow against the Dukes while they were engaged in marrying off Alma, but they'd only bagged one Duke, and had taken something of a mauling in the process. The spectacle of a stranger handling his horse as though it belonged to him wasn't calculated to improve the Giant's disposition. Added to that, he believed strongly that his remarkable size afforded him certain privileges and advantages, which others in the Mesa Hills area didn't enjoy.

That was how he came to tell Morgan Latimer to, 'Git your filthy paws off my horse, you dirty, good for nothing horse thief!'

For the second time in five minutes, Morgan Latimer's eyes glinted like sparks coming off a chunk of flint as the man-mountain loomed over him.

'Horse thief?' he challenged. 'Mister, I borrowed this nag last night while a bunch of dirty dry-gulchers were busy shooting up a place where there was at least one helpless female, and one innocent bystander, namely me. And if this horse belongs to you, then that means you were one of those dirty dry-gulchers. Would that be right?'

The Giant's bushy black eyebrows descended ponderously. 'Who are you, big mouth?'

Latimer jerked a thumb towards the groggy figure being helped down the street by two passersby.

'Me? I'm the man who just busted that son of a bitch for interfering in my life. I've got a feelin' that you're buckin' for a dose of the same — you mountain of lard!'

It took a couple of seconds for the Giant to understand that he'd been both challenged and insulted, but far less time to launch himself into a low dive, the speed of which took Morgan Latimer by surprise and saw him hurled into the dust with over 300 pounds of man atop him.

Badly winded, all Latimer could do was use his head again and he did so with some success. The Giant's head snapped back from the impact of the blow and Latimer's elbow smashed him in the jaw and he rolled out from under the man. A huge arm slammed across his face and he saw stars, flashes of lights, and heard loud ringing.

The Giant was no pushover. In fact, he hit like a horse kicked.

Morgan Latimer spat some blood, rolled away from another mighty blow and staggered to his feet, grinning. This was just what he wanted. A good dust-up to burn his full head of steam.

'He'll beat you to a pulp, Mr Latimer,' an amiable voice called as the Giant sprang to his feet, wiping blood from his gashed brow. 'I'd hightail it if I was you.'

Jason Kirby wasn't Morgan Latimer.

As the two stood toe to toe slugging it out, with neither giving an inch, a sizeable crowd gathered, and it was interesting to observe how a town sickened by the previous night's violence could actually enjoy a good, honest knockdown-drag-out brawl where the worst that could happen would be somebody getting knocked out.

The Giant threw a right cross. Latimer retaliated with two slamming straight left jabs. This was followed with an upper-cut, a rip, a knee to the groin and an elbow to the teeth.

As the sheriff shouldered his way through the swelling mob, Jason Kirby grabbed him by the shoulder.

'Hey, don't be a spoilsport, Sheriff,' he chuckled. 'This is worth the admission money. My partner Mr

Latimer is about twice as tough as he looks. Let 'em go.'

'I've had enough of this drifter!' Stark snapped, pulling free. 'He wants to beat up on everyone.' He reached for the brawlers. 'Stop this at once!'

He grabbed Latimer's shirt just as the Giant threw a haymaker. Latimer ducked instinctively. A fist the size of a normal man's head caught the sheriff of El Paso squarely on the chin. He dropped like a sack of wheat.

It was about then that Latimer and the Giant both seemed to reach the same decision at the same time: their dust-up had gone far enough.

Staggering a little and leaking some blood, Morgan Latimer untied his strawberry roan and turned to the crowd. Wordlessly they opened up to let him through. The fight had done the trick. He wasn't mad anymore.

Well, maybe just a little.

11

Insects were buzzing in swarms. The relentless droning invaded the tranquility of the sheriff's dreams. He groaned a protest and tried to nestle into the jailhouse bench where he had been stretched out to recover. His forehead bumped the wood paneling and he frowned in pain. The buzzing rose to a crescendo and suddenly he sat up, wide-eyed and sweating to stare into the hideously enlarged faces of a bumblebee and praying mantis, which, to his utter relief, quickly settled down into the familiar features of citizens Denson and Gilpin.

'What happened?' Sheriff Abel Stark wanted to know.

They told him, and then drifted out onto the jailhouse porch while Stark got himself together.

Half a block along the street, a tall

figure was tying a strawberry roan to the hotel hitch rail.

'What do you make of him?' Denson, although thoroughly unimpressive physically, had a way of speaking that carried weight.

The sheriff was still counting his lucky stars to have gotten away from the Duke compound the previous night only minutes after the shooting started. He was not physically a match to take on Latimer either in hand-to-hand combat; this he knew too well now.

'I still reckon he's just a dodgy drifter, Mr Denson. Dime a dozen, Latimer's breed.'

'He's tough.'

'So's all that breed.'

'He's gritty.'

The sheriff looked at the older man, who only recently had added him to his payroll.

'What are you trying to say, Mr Denson?'

'Not sure. But we might be able to make use of him if he stays around,'

Russell Denson replied.

'And if he stays alive.'

'That too. Keep an eye on him for me, will you, Stark?'

'Whatever you want, Mr Denson,' the sheriff replied obediently.

⋆   ⋆   ⋆

Fleecy white clouds drifted leisurely over the sunny Mesa Hills as the Duke clan prepared to attend the burial of cousin Elmer. Black suits hung on the clothes line, getting rid of the pervading odor of mothballs. Boiled white shirts were critically examined; rifle barrels were polished until they gleamed. No Duke in his right mind would attend a funeral without his rifle. There was a ritual to buryings in the Mesa Hills, and the right and the necessity to bear arms was part of it.

'You can't go to a funeral like that!' declared Clayton Duke as his sister appeared in her solemn finest.

'Why not?' Alma asked innocently, looking down.

Clayton snorted disgustedly. For men who drank, fought and raised Cain with rare dedication, they were a prudish lot. 'Daddy,' he said, 'will you tell Alma what is wrong with that there dress she's wearin'?'

Clifton Duke sat on a cane chair in the sun while people brought him various pieces of apparel, which he was slowly putting on as he brooded on recent events and composed in his mind suitable segments of sarcasm to mark the occasion.

'What?' he said grumpily. He scowled at his daughter. 'It's too blamed low, is what is wrong with it, Alma.'

Alma, who had sat up late lowering the bodice of her only black dress to make it more interesting, stamped her foot.

'You don't want anyone to notice me!' she cried.

'They'll not only notice you iffen you wore that to a buryin',' intoned her father, 'they'd arrest you. Go fix it up decent, girl.'

'I'll never get a husband!' Alma yelled, rushing off.

The girl badly wanted to marry, although not necessarily for romantic reasons. Mainly, she wanted to get away from her family. Anybody in their right mind would, if they belonged to a family like the Dukes. But even though comely enough and generously endowed, as her updated mourning dress revealed all too clearly, she was still unmarried. It seemed she couldn't even get a husband at the end of a gun barrel and she was getting desperate.

'Women!' Grant snapped, doing his black string tie before a small square of mirror propped up on a windowsill. He turned to the others. 'How does it look?'

'You look like an undertaker,' replied young Levi.

'Better than lookin' like a donkey's ass,' Grant shot back.

The clan wasn't at its best today. The

fresh bullet holes in the woodwork around them in the breezeway were mute reminders of last night and everything about it had gone wrong. To cap things off, Obadiah had just arrived back with a swelling on his jaw the size of a pigeon's egg, after a public licking at the hands of the drifter who had made them all look silly. And now they were faced with the prospect of attending the funeral of a clansman which would drive home to the whole county the fact that they'd run second to another clash with the enemy.

It wasn't a good day — not a good day at all.

Clifton Duke sat in the sunlight for a long time after he'd finished dressing. Attired in a somber black suit, boiled white shirt, string tie and greased boots, the clan head looked almost impressive. It was only when he jammed his floppy hat low over his ears and took up his shotgun that he looked as mean as a stick-poked rattler.

There had been a time after his

sensible wife had left him, when Clifton Duke had actually set out to win himself another woman to warm his bed at night and help him raise his brood. But the woman he'd wanted hadn't wanted him, which was something he still found hard to comprehend. He didn't bother about women any longer, although he'd never really forgotten that particular woman. In the Mesa Hills, it was impossible to forget her, things being as they were.

Still, romance wasn't what was occupying the mind of Clifton Duke at the moment as he sat soaking up the warm sunshine. Nor was he thinking about work, business, family, his health or even of the long, lean drifter who had compromised his daughter. He wasn't even thinking about his late nephew, except in a roundabout way.

What preoccupied this violent old man as he stroked his whiskers and cleaned his nails with a clasp knife was the squaring of accounts.

'An eye for an eye!' he suddenly said. 'That's what the good book says!'

Everybody paused in what they were doing, and immediately began looking happier. This was the sort of talk the Dukes had been reared on.

'When, Pa?' Levi asked eagerly. 'At the funeral?'

One quality Levi Duke didn't lack was enthusiasm. He was perennially ready for battle with the Filmores at any place, and for any reason.

'Not there, dammit, boy!' Clifton Duke chided. 'Don't you have any respect for the dead?'

'The Filmores will all be there,' Levi pointed out darkly.

'That don't count for nothin',' Clifton chided again. 'Iffen we start shootin' folks at buryin's, pretty soon we'll have nobody turnin' up for nobody.'

Grant Duke gave his father a knowing look. 'And that'd be no good on account of we'd miss a chance to see Narcissa Filmore now and then.

Wouldn't we, Pa?'

Although the significance of this weighted remark was lost on the younger Dukes, Clifton certainly knew what his hulking eldest son was alluding to. He put on a look like thunder.

'Iffen mouth was grit, you'd wipe the yard with that pack single-handed last night, boy,' he rasped. 'Too bad it didn't turn out that way, ain't it?'

Grant stood reproved. 'So, what's this about an eye fer an eye?' he asked bad-temperedly.

'After the drifter busted loose and made us foolish,' Clifton said, 'we jest cain't afford to let the Filmores git away with wipin' out cousin Elmer. Iffen we don't git at least one of them to balance things out, we'll be the laughin' stock of the valley.'

As usual, Clifton Duke was tending to exaggerate a little. No matter how many reverses they suffered, nobody was likely to laugh the Dukes down; nobody could afford to take that sort of risk. But he'd made his point. Pride was all to the Dukes, and that pride had taken a severe mauling over the past twenty-four hours. Redress was top priority.

'What about afterwards?' ventured Obadiah, still a little glassy-eyed, but always able to rally at a whiff of mayhem. 'Everybody will be drinking, same as they do after every plantin'. Should be any number of chances for us tonight.'

'I'd like to get Garrett Filmore, by God,' Clayton said with feeling. His left arm was in a calico sling. The El Paso doctor had dug a .44 slug out of his shoulder in a daybreak operation. Clayton Duke believed the man responsible was Garrett Filmore, with whom he had been carrying on a feud for years.

'Boy's a bigger bastard,' countered Grant, cracking his knuckles and scowling balefully.

'Mebbe I'll get a crack at him.'

'Hell, let's think bigger,' ventured Levi. 'Why don't we set our sights on her?'

There was a silence, thick and immutable, as Clifton Duke turned an icy stare on his youngest son.

'You talkin' about Narcissa Filmore, boy?' he asked ominously.

Levi looked perplexed. 'Of course. Who else would I be talkin' 'bout?' Then he grinned. 'I sure as shootin' wouldn't be suggesting we start in pluggin' them gals, would I? Not them pretty pair. But that old lady must be ripe to get her comeuppance . . . ' His voice faded under his father's frosty glare and he added uncertainly. 'Don't you reckon', Pa?'

Grant gave his brother a big nudge and a warning look. 'We ain't low enough to start shootin' up women yet,' he growled. Then he brightened. 'Hey, how about the Giant? That oversized tub of lard was up here burnin' gunpowder like a man with four hands last night. He's got it comin'.'

'That drifter was beatin' up the Giant after he king-hit me this mornin',' Obadiah said, tenderly rubbing his king-sized bruise. His eyes widened at a thought. 'Say, if Latimer has got it in for the Giant, maybe we could talk him into rubbin' him out for us?'

'We Dukes bag our own varmints,' Clifton Duke said irritably. Then he fell silent as his daughter reappeared. The neckline of the offending dress was now exaggeratedly high, right up to the chin.

'Is this all right?' Alma asked sarcastically. 'Or should I wear a muffler as well?'

'Don't get sassy with me, girl,' Clifton warned, getting to his feet. 'I know what's best for you. Where's my shotgun?'

Clayton produced the weapon, which the old man accepted lovingly, running gnarled hands along the polished stock as he watched the sunlight glint on the metal baseplate.

'It's time we was leavin' fer town,' he announced. 'And you boys think on what I said.'

'What did you say?' Alma pouted and pursed her lips.

'Nothin' for a girl to know,' her father responded.

'I never get told anything,' she protested. 'You treat me like a little kid, Pa.'

Duke looked her over. She was built like a full-blown woman should be built.

'Well, you certainly ain't that,' he conceded. He wagged a finger. 'And no flirtin' in town today, you hear? Only for your flirty ways, cousin Elmer would be alive today.'

Alma rolled her eyes. Her mother had a lot to answer for in running away, she thought. Alma always blamed the incident for her father's twisted and prudish ideas about women. She knew she had been the innocent party in last night's drama, but Clifton Duke didn't believe there was any such thing as an innocent woman.

12

Morgan Latimer rode his strawberry roan across the valley's parkland, making a wide circuit, and crossed the Rio Grande at the rift, and then swept a curve back to the general direction of El Paso.

A mile from the valley entrance, long, forested slopes tumbled down to the gorge where the river formed a water-fall-like effect. Beyond, oak and pine trees fringed the green land: pretty country by any yardstick, yet empty. Latimer had barely sighted a soul since setting out on his ride, which was designed to work the kinks and tensions out of his long frame and give his horse a workout. He had ridden by abandoned ranch houses, at least one or two of which looked as though they'd been quit in a hurry and recently.

A man could settle in a place like

this, he mused. Then he frowned at a thought. Providing, of course, he wasn't averse to gun smoke.

It was no mystery why Mission Valley and the Mesa Hills were almost deserted, while every second business house over in El Paso was boarded up. The War was over, but something akin to war was still being fought in El Paso County.

Several miles eastward of Latimer's position, where massive oak forests marked the borders of canyons, the Filmore clan was traveling the dusty road to town to attend the funeral of Elmer Duke. The women, Narcissa and her twin daughters, Lena and Tara, sat soberly in the covered carriage while the men riding behind argued among themselves over who could rightly lay claim to having the 'honor', but they couldn't agree about it, and the debate threatened to continue all the way to El Paso.

Ten miles south, coming down through the pretty Mesa Valley foothills from their compound, the Dukes were also on the road, while in the town itself, the saloons were doing a roaring trade catering for the mourners. Prominent amongst the serious drinkers was the man who would be officiating at the ceremony, the Reverend Uriah Redden, who, one way or another, was having a busy week of it.

Up at the ceremony, three gravediggers rested on their shovels in the shade of a tree beside a six by six hole. Gravedigging was a steady job in El Paso, and these men, along with the undertaker, were among the very few who didn't care if the feud never ended.

Another with the same attitude was the ugly, wealthy man who drove past the cemetery on his way from his handsome house on the hill that overlooked the town to his Main Street office.

Russell Denson lived alone and didn't like it. He had his own secret reasons for wanting to see the feud continued along the bloody course it had been following for several years, but because he was a solitary man with no close friends, nobody had an inkling of what they might be.

Russell would attend the ceremony, even though he had always regarded the deceased as a poisonous little jerk who should have been pitched down a well at birth. He wore his best gray suit and his expensive blood-red boots had been buffed until they shone like mirrors. Funerals and weddings were the major social events in these parts.

When Morgan Latimer reached the crest of a rise, which brought the rooftops of the distant town into sight, he reined in to roll a cigarette and do some serious thinking.

As he built the smoke, he noted his skinned knuckles. He ached from head to toe as a result of all the violence and exertion. Ordinarily, he would not have objected, but felt he'd had more than enough of trouble in El Paso County. He suspected that the real reason he'd gone riding following his dust-ups with the Giant and Obadiah Duke was to reach a decision about staying or going.

He was still searching for peace, he told himself, and it was a sure bet he wouldn't find it here.

He lit his cigarette and drew deep. It was a great pity that this lovely valley with its protecting ring of wooded hills was such a hotbed of trouble. Otherwise, he just might have found enough reasons to stay on for a spell and see what happened.

His gaze focused on the town. There was nothing to be gained by his hanging around any longer just to show everyone that he couldn't be forced to move against his will, he reflected. He'd already made that point. They said there was good cow country over to the southwest beyond the Mesa Hills and even into Mexico. Maybe he'd be luckier there.

The resolution was hardening as he headed for the distant ribbon of trail winding up from the north. Head out. Good decision. Leave the Dukes and

Filmores to their bloody games. Maybe only when there was none of them left to pull a trigger, he thought sardonically, would they realize just how bloody-minded and stupid they had been.

As Latimer rode onto the trail from a grassy draw, he saw the cavalcade coming towards him, heading in the same direction he was. There was a carriage and pair with some nine or ten riders. The women in the carriage were decked out in finery, while the horsemen all wore hats, coats and ties. It was only when he identified two of the riders, the Giant and Theo Filmore that Latimer guessed who they were.

Moving onto the shoulder of the trail, Morgan Latimer turned his roan to face the oncoming travelers, and rested his hand on his gun butt.

He didn't trust anybody here, especially people who'd been trying to kill him the previous night, even though they may not have been aware of it.

They could go ahead; he didn't want

a pack of Filmores behind him.

Theo Filmore recognized him and came spurring ahead of the carriage, followed by his twin brother. The two reined in to eye Latimer curiously.

'Howdy, bridegroom,' Theo quipped.

'Real funny,' Latimer shot back. 'You always attend funerals of the folks you kill, do you, Filmore?'

'Mostly.' Theo was noncommittal. 'What are you doin' way out here?'

'Mindin' my own business.' Latimer fell silent as the carriage came abreast and drew to a halt. He found himself being examined by a handsome, stern-faced woman with silver hair, and two pretty daughters, obviously twins.

'Who is this?' Narcissa Filmore demanded. They told her, and she gave Latimer a sternly disapproving look. 'So, you're the hellion responsible for last night's uproar, are you, sir? I must say you look the type.'

Morgan Latimer said clearly, 'I didn't murder anyone, which is more than I can say for your clan, ma'am.'

'Murder's not the word you're lookin' for, Latimer,' Garrett Filmore retorted.

'Don't pay him no mind,' advised the Giant. 'This drifter's got a loose mouth.'

'I'd have loosened more than your mouth if we'd finished what we started earlier,' Latimer retorted. But his words lacked real force. He was distracted by the twin girls. Or more correctly, by the taller and darker of the pair — the one with eyes the color of violets.

'Come along, boys,' Narcissa Filmore snapped. 'I believe we've seen enough of Mr Latimer.'

'Oh, don't be so hard on the poor man, Mother,' said the girl with the violet eyes. 'He doesn't look so terrible to me.' She smiled. 'Are you going to the funeral, Mr Latimer?'

'No,' he replied, removing his hat. 'Leastwise, I wasn't . . . '

'Nobody misses a good funeral in the valley,' said her sister. Both girls seemed to be taking the whole business of a

147

funeral with a very light touch. 'You might as well travel with us if you're going that way. Don't you think so, Tara?'

So that was her name: Tara. Morgan Latimer had no idea why it should seem so important for him to know it, yet it was for some reason.

'Of course,' Tara said with a twinkle. 'Any friend of the Giant's is a friend of ours.'

'Girls!' Narcissa Filmore said with compressed lips, her back ramrod-erect. 'What a trial they can be!' She tapped the driver with her parasol. 'Drive on, James. Let's get there if we're going.'

As the carriage rolled off with the riders following it, Theo Filmore held back. A handsome man with a good cut of jaw and square shoulders, he looked Morgan Latimer up and down.

'So, how do we rate you, drifter?' he challenged. 'Friend or foe?'

'Neither,' came the reply. 'I came here neutral and I mean to stay that way if you and the Dukes just let me be.'

'Come on, Theo!' Garrett yelled, swinging his arm.

Theo Filmore reached a decision.

'Well, you can travel in with us if you want. But I'll be watchin' you real close like.'

Latimer might have told him to go straight to hell, but he figured they were already there, and if it had not been for the girl. He wanted to see more of Miss Tara Filmore, and suddenly found himself wishing he'd worn the better of his two shirts for the ride.

'I'll be watchin' you too,' he grunted.

'Suits me fine.'

They set off together and caught up with the main party as it topped a low green hill. Pushing his horse past several riders, who eyed him suspiciously, Latimer fell in alongside the carriage. Narcissa Filmore glared. Lena shrugged. Tara Filmore gave him a smile.

Long before they were rolling down

the main street of El Paso twenty minutes later, Morgan Latimer suspected he might be having second thoughts about leaving.

Although peace could be a mighty rare commodity to find, it wasn't half as rare as a girl with sparkling violet eyes.

13

There was an unwritten understanding between the Dukes and the Filmores that their feud should not spill over into El Paso itself. It was perfectly all right for them to shoot, strangle, maim, hang, drown, abuse, insult and commit plunder and pillage against one another in the valley and the surrounding hills, but not in the town itself. There had to be a neutral territory in every war, and El Paso was it for the warring families of El Paso County.

But despite this arrangement, the families avoided each other as much as possible on those rare occasions when they visited the town at the same time. As a rule, the Filmores frequented the Silver Dollar hotel while the Dukes relaxed at the bar of the Golden Dawn saloon.

From the gallery of the hotel where

he'd occupied a nice comfortable rocker just on sundown, Morgan Latimer continued to watch and observe as the early night took over. He told himself he'd chosen this spot because it was the best observation point on the street, but deep down, he wasn't sure that his choice might have been influenced by the hope of catching another look at Tara Filmore.

The walks drummed to the thud of boot heels as piano music, rough laughter and the clink of glassware spilled from the town's three saloons.

From time to time, Filmores, Dukes and their various allies and relatives passed the Silver Dollar. Latimer also saw Sheriff Abel Stark on several occasions. The lawman looked tense, for although there was no sign of trouble as of yet, it was always a possibility with so many people who hated one another in town at the same time.

Latimer could feel the tension. If the families didn't butt heads here in El

Paso tonight, he sensed it wouldn't be long before they would.

He straightened as he saw two familiar figures mounting the steps at the far end of the gallery. Alma Duke held her father's arm, and Clifton Duke was minus his shotgun.

The pair was making for the doors when Alma sighted Morgan Latimer seated in the shadows. She halted, smiled and gave a hesitant wave.

'Hiya, Morgan,' she called. 'You lonely?'

'I'm fine,' Latimer replied. 'How was the funeral?'

'It was lovely, for the occasion.'

'Goin' visitin'?' he asked curiously.

'Sure am. I'm calling on Tara and Lena. We're friends despite everything, you know.'

Clifton Duke stood, stony-faced and rigid, staring straight at Morgan Latimer, who gave him look for look. For some reason, the mean old bastard didn't seem to object to visiting the enemy camp, Latimer

153

thought. That didn't make a lot of sense, but few things here rarely did.

'Well, nice seein' you, Alma,' Latimer said, thinking to himself she probably was a truly nice gal, except for her family. 'Under more relaxed circumstances, that is.'

'I figgered you'd have been smart enough to get out of town by now, drifter,' Clifton Duke said, breaking his silence. 'I haven't fergot what happened along the crick . . . '

'Oh, Pa, how many times do I have to tell you that nothing happened?' Alma sounded almost disappointed. She tugged at her father's arm. 'Come on now, we're not having any arguments tonight.'

'Women!' Clifton Duke snorted as they disappeared. 'Nothing but trouble.'

Twisting in his chair, Latimer looked through the window and saw the Dukes making their way to the corner of the lobby where Narcissa Filmore, her daughters and several of their clan and allies were holding court. Clifton Duke actually bowed. The world was full of surprises.

Another presented itself in short time later when the arrival of a fast-speeding wagon sent pedestrians scattering wildly in all directions. In the process of rolling a cigarette, Latimer looked up to see the driver standing in the rig and urging his team along at full notch. Drunk or out of his mind, Latimer reflected, as the vehicle came closer. Maybe both.

As the racing wagon approached the Silver Dollar, the driver's big boot kicked the brake. The wheels locked, smoke rose from scorching leather, and the wagon lurched and swayed to a dust-churning halt directly before the hotel steps, where the driver sprang to the ground almost before the wheels had stopped turning.

'Whew!' roared Jason Kirby, waving his hat and charging up the steps. 'I'm one part ring-tailed alligator, four parts snappin' turtle and — '

'And too darn noisy,' barked Latimer. 'So simmer down, would ya?'

Kirby slammed to a halt and swung belligerently towards the sound of the voice, his vision somewhat impaired by alcohol fumes. ' . . . and two parts fightin' grizzly!' he finished, lunging forward. 'Get on your miserable feet and . . . ' He jerked to a halt. 'Well, I be tar and feathered! Latimer! Why didn't you say so?' He pulled a bottle from his hip pocket. 'Have a drink, pardner. I'm celebratin' tonight.'

Latimer accepted the bottle, but didn't drink.

'Celebrating what exactly?' Latimer enquired.

'Bein' alive, for Pete's sake!' Kirby hurled his lean body into a chair and slapped Latimer's back. 'Can you come up with a better reason?'

Morgan Latimer's rare smile appeared. He realized Kirby was only a little drunk. His exuberance was mainly due to exhilaration. Latimer had rarely encountered anybody so full of life.

Kirby calmed down some as they sat

talking and smoking. He pulled his .44 when they glimpsed Obadiah and Grant Duke coming their way, but Latimer restrained him.

'I don't figure they're looking for trouble,' Latimer cautioned, pointing with this thumb over his shoulder. 'Their old man is inside.'

'He is?' Kirby peered inside to see Clifton Duke and Alma just leaving. He didn't speak as they emerged and joined Obadiah and Grant by the steps. The brothers bent dark looks on Latimer, but at a word from their father, the group set off along the street. Alma turned and waved goodbye to Latimer.

'Well, I'll be . . . ' Kirby chuckled, leaning back in his chair. 'Visitin' with Narcissa, eh? Must be a flicker of the old fire still left, I reckon.'

'What are you talkin' about?' Latimer was now watching Sheriff Stark as he circled Kirby's wagon and team, which was blocking off direct entry to the hotel.

'Him,' Kirby said, pointing after Clifton Duke's receding figure. 'You see, after his wife left him, that mean old cuss set his cap at Narcissa Filmore, her bein' a handsome widower and all. It never came to nothin', of course, Duke bein' lower'n a snake's belly and all, and her something of a lady, even if she would blow a man's head off quick as look at him. But I've heard whispers from time to time that the rotten old polecat is still pining for Narcissa, and what we just seen might prove that.' He gave Latimer a rough nudge. 'I just love gossip, Latimer. Yessir, gossipin' and winnin' wagon races, that's what keeps my boilers steamin'.'

The argument began as soon as the sheriff climbed the steps to order Kirby to remove his wagon. As the debate looked like being somewhat long-winded, Latimer left them to it and went inside in the hope of treating Tara Filmore to a cup of coffee in the hotel's dining room.

The Filmores, Theo and Garrett,

were drinking at the small bar in the adjoining room with some of their henchmen, and Latimer noticed that some of them were beginning to show the effects of the alcohol. He had also noticed, a short time before, that none of the Dukes he'd seen seemed to have been drinking at all.

Curious, but hardly important, he mused.

Morgan Latimer put on his best smile for Tara Filmore.

14

The moon was bright at midnight as Marcus Fowler made his slow way home from town. A second cousin of the Filmore boys, and a harness maker by trade, young Marcus lived with his mother up by the ravine in a spacious ranch house. The house had been abandoned by an Irish family who'd quit the Mesa Hills in a big hurry in the middle of the night about a year or so earlier when two Dukes and three or four Filmores had shot it out with pistols and rifles in their horse corral.

Music accompanied Marcus on the way home and helped make light of the miles. He was a more than fine harmonica player, and had entertained the folks around the Filmore household with sad and sentimental songs about dying cowboys until the whiskey had caught up with him and friends had

160

persuaded him to head home while he was still capable of sitting a saddle.

The tune he played as he rode at a walk towards the creek crossing was 'Bury Me Not on the Lone Prairie'. It was sad as hell but Marcus was fighting back a big grin as he snorted the lyrics, dropping the harmonica from his mouth to sing, 'O bury me not on the lone prairie/ These words came low and mournfully/ From the pallid lips of the youth who lay/ On his dying bed at the close of day.' He had been up at the Duke ranch and compound the previous night and entertained a strong suspicion that it had been his shot — his bullet — that had brought to an end the short and undistinguished life of Elmer Duke.

'Couldn't have happened to a nicer sinner,' he grinned, banging the harmonica against the heel of his hand to clean the reeds.

Tree shadows lay across the road ahead like black pits. On the left, a tributary of the Rio Grande bubbled over its rocky bed on its way to join up with the main stream. A light breeze fanned the oak trees, which shone and shimmered in the moonlight. On the right rose a steep slope, littered with boulders and scarred by an old avalanche. A large, plump brown owl flew overhead, on the hunt.

Marcus Fowler was feeling no pain as he racked his memory for yet another appropriate selection to mark a burying day. He'd had a fine time with his kinfolk, and even though there had been no crowing over Elmer Duke's death, the mood had been good. They might have failed to notch up the full-blooded victory they had hoped for when they set out for the Duke compound, but at least they had come out of the battle ahead and unscathed.

He lifted the harmonica to his lips and the doleful strains of 'The Campfire had gone out' floated up the boulder-littered slope to reach the ears of the men straining on the ten foot long log lever they had wedged underneath a chunk of granite as big as a buckboard wagon.

Sweating and grunting, the toilers were making considerable noise, but a combination of harmonica music, the stream, the breeze in the trees and the gutful of whiskey that Marcus Fowler had put away, which caused his head to buzz like a fallen hornet's nest, guaranteed that he heard nothing at all until it was too late.

It was already too late when the buckboard-sized boulder gave up the struggle of trying to cling to the edge of the slope, and began turning end over end as it fell downwards.

Sparks flew as it smashed into another boulder, which in turn came loose, taking a great deal of soil and gravel with it.

By the time Marcus realized his danger, half the slope was on the move. He screamed but nobody heard him above the rumbling roar of the sliding boulder. Tall trees snapped off with sounds like rifle shots and tons of rocky rubble boiled all the way down across the trail and into the creek before it even looked like losing any momentum.

All that remained visible of Marcus Fowler when the first riders came by at daybreak the next morning was his little harmonica, gleaming brightly atop the massive pile of stones and earth.

The townsfolk had to dig to find the rest of him.

★   ★   ★

All over El Paso, in every type of house, there could be heard the sound of coat hangers clicking as the citizens took out their funeral garb which they had used only a few days earlier: for Elmer Duke on Wednesday, now Marcus Fowler on Saturday. The gravediggers were starting to complain of being overworked.

The notice lodged by the Filmore family on behalf of Marcus's distraught mother had said nothing about hate, feuds or bloody murder. It read:

FOWLER, Marcus. Very suddenly. Beloved son of Martha Fowler. Dear friend of Narcissa, Theo, Garrett, Lena and Tara Filmore, and of all their many friends, family and relations. May his memory live on. Interment 3 p.m. Saturday.

'Poor Marcus,' a saloon girl at the Silver Dollar said, wiping away tears, when she read the notice. 'He was a sweet man.'

'He was a dirty little back-shootin', lying, cheatin', whore-chastin' son of a . . . ' disagreed Levi Duke, who had played no small part in dumping a thousand tons of country-side on Marcus's head.

'Maybe you're right about that,' the fickle girl replied, and dried her eyes before heading back upstairs to take out her best and only black dress — once again.

It seemed that while there would be a big crowd to see Marcus off, he would be genuinely missed by relatively few in the area. Indeed, the only significant aspect of Marcus's violent demise seemed to be the fact that the Dukes had repaid the Filmores for Elmer Duke.

Nobody really believed that the avalanche had been a natural occurrence.

★   ★   ★

Funds were running mighty thin.

Morgan Latimer counted out some change to pay for a beer, and then carried it to the end of the bar where he commanded a good view of the El Paso town street.

He hadn't been there all that long when Ambrose Orton sauntered in. Following the unseemly incident with Alma Duke out along Willow Creek several days earlier, old Ambrose had been lying lower than a snake, fearful that the Dukes might learn the true story of what had happened and come after him.

On the other hand, the Dukes plainly had too many things on their plate to worry about the likes of Ambrose Orton's whereabouts, and he was again out and about in his new job as assistant to Russell Denson.

He was nearly rendered speechless when Morgan Latimer gave him a slight nod and an almost genuine smile.

'Howdy,' Latimer greeted. 'Want a drink?'

One couldn't blame Ambrose Orton for being a little leery of the offer. Morgan Latimer had quickly earned a reputation in El Paso, and after seeing him in action against two of the valley's toughest characters in Obadiah Duke and the Giant, Ambrose really wanted no part of the drifter. But because Latimer seemed amiable enough, he accepted the offer of a drink and quickly found out the reason behind the offer.

The drifter was looking for work, and it was a well-known fact that Russell Denson was one of the few people in the region capable of employing any-body looking for work.

'As far as I know, there's nothing offering at the moment,' Ambrose Orton declared.

'You could mention my name to Mr Denson,' Latimer said clearly.

'Maybe I could.' Ambrose Orton was feeling cockier than normal as he went along. 'What can you do?' He grinned. 'Aside from raise hell and whatnot.'

Latimer was serious. 'Break horses, herd cattle, any cowboyin' job, a little blacksmithing, can handle just about any sort of job a ranch or the West has to offer . . . I can drive anything with wheels. Guess that about sums it up.'

Ambrose Orton sipped his drink. 'Have you tried the Filmores, Latimer?'

Latimer looked at him sharply. 'What? Um . . . no.'

Ambrose Orton smiled slyly. 'We are family . . . distant family, of course, but I've heard you've been gettin' kind of friendly with them out there at the canyon. One in particular, from what I hear. One lovely young lady to be precise.'

This man was treading on dangerous ground, for despite all his protestations about searching for peace and quiet, Morgan Latimer could be a pretty prickly character when it came to certain matters. He considered giving Ambrose Orton a strip of his tongue for his smart remark, but remembering his financial situation, he decided against it.

'Reckon I should go to the man himself, Mr Denson, instead. You know, get it straight from the horse's mouth,' was all he said.

'No, I'll let him know that you are asking.'

'Fine.'

Morgan Latimer drained the remaining beer from his glass and promptly left.

As he headed along the main street for the livery, a heavily laden wagon swung in from the east trail, packed high with furniture and humanity.

Migrants.

As Latimer paused to roll a cigarette, the sheriff emerged from his office, donning his hat. Abel Stark wore a haggard look these days. People were being killed at an alarming rate, and as always seemed to be the case, there was no clear-cut indication as to the guilty parties.

The lawman had his eye on the approaching wagon until he caught sight of Latimer. The two men had been wary of each other ever since the shootout at the Duke compound. The sheriff approached the tall drifter warily.

'Still hanging around town I see, Mr Latimer.'

'Sure looks that way, Sheriff.'

'Reckoned you'd moved on further west by now. Not thinkin' of moving on just yet?'

'Maybe I've taken a certain liking to this place,' Latimer said with the slightest hint of a grin.

Abel Stark glanced away to hide his

disappointment. As the sheriff, he felt he had more than enough troublemakers in the feuding families without adding more in the shape of this drifter, this outsider — Morgan Latimer.

The wagoner rolled his rig to a halt when he saw the badge of Abel Stark. He was grizzled, red-eyed, thick-bodied and coated in layers of dust.

'Is this Santa Teresa, Marshal?' the driver of the wagon asked.

'It's Sheriff, and no, you have the wrong town,' Stark said. 'Santa Teresa lies just beyond the valley to the west a bit.' He put on a politician's smile. 'But you folks are more than welcome to stay a spell in El Paso.'

'El Paso?' The man's wife spoke now. She looked alarmed as she gazed around the town. 'Is this El Paso?'

'Sure enough is, ma'am,' said Stark. 'We have plenty of land for homesteading, good water, and — '

'And fighting,' the woman broke in. 'We've heard about this place a hundred miles back, didn't we, William?

People are calling the place Hell Paso.'

The wagon's driver looked grave. 'Sure enough did. And we've heard more coming across the badlands too. You folks have had more killings here just this past week.' He sounded aggrieved, like he was holding the lawman personally responsible. 'Ain't that so?'

The sheriff tried to talk his way around the charge, but there was no way he could do so. There was no arguing with corpses. He did his best to get the couple off the subject of the feud and onto the more attractive topics of land and climate, but they simply refused to give any thought to those and did not listen. They were on their way to Santa Teresa.

'Maybe we will continue on to Arizona to put some distance between ourselves and this town,' the driver added.

Just as fast as they had come into town, they had left the town.

Morgan Latimer was finishing off his

smoke as the rig rumbled away, with two ragged kids sitting atop the rocking load. 'Nice town,' he drawled. 'Too bad nobody wants to stay in it.'

Sheriff Stark rounded on him. 'It seems to me you can share some of the blame for that, Mr Latimer. Things were quiet before you turned up and interfered with Alma Duke.'

'I didn't interfere with anybody! Especially Alma Duke!'

Stark sighed heavily. 'Ah, maybe you didn't at that.' He sighed once more as he lowered himself to a nearby porch bench. 'I'm tired, Mr Latimer, and getting more tired as the time goes by. In case you don't know it, trying to keep a community afloat when it's doing its damnedest to sink is no easy job. Maybe it's impossible, who knows?'

Latimer almost felt sorry for the man. He looked both ways along the main street. At the moment, in the wake of the departing potential homesteaders, it looked long, wide, bleak, and empty. The only splash of color was the calico sign advertising the wagon race.

'Jason Kirby tells me you're expecting a lot of people to turn up for the wagon race,' Morgan Latimer said. 'Maybe that'll give El Paso the boost it needs.'

'The way things are going,' Sheriff Stark said wearily, 'some poor clown will fall out of his rig and get run over. If that happens, I suppose folks will lay the blame at my feet or on the feud.' He gloomily considered his own words for a while, and then glanced up. 'Do you aim to still be in town on race day?'

'I could be. Why?'

'Do you drive, Mr Latimer?'

'Yeah. Why you asking?'

'Don't be so damned suspicious, drifter. Just thought it might be a way you could make a few dollars, is all.'

Morgan Latimer's pride was stung. 'Are you saying I'm broke?'

The sheriff gave up. 'Goodbye, Mr Latimer,' he said, walking off. 'I hope when I next take a turn of the street I'll find you gone — for good, that is.'

Latimer was gone when Sheriff Stark emerged an hour later.

But not for good.

15

The racing wagon bowled down the slope at breakneck speed and took the corner at the bottom on two wheels, forcing Latimer to lean far out over the passenger's side to assist the balance. They seemed to travel about fifty yards before the raised wheels came back to earth with a spine-rattling crunch. Roaring and cursing, Jason Kirby applied the whip, the horses hurtled around the next corner in a surging boil of dust, then ran straight, and hard for the 'finish line', which was the large oak tree standing in front of the Kirby cabin.

As Kirby finally dragged his team to a halt some hundred or so yards farther on, a shot rang out from the cabin and a startled Morgan Latimer heard something whistle overhead. Dropping low, he looked back to see Kirby's wife standing on the porch, holding a smoking Winchester rifle.

'That'll do for today!' she bellowed. 'You're dusting my washing.'

'Whatever you say, dear!' Kirby hollered back.

Latimer rose slowly, staring. 'Whatever you say?' he bounced back. Was this Jason Kirby, the wild man, speaking?

Kirby looked embarrassed as he gently turned the rig and guided the foam-lathered horses back towards the headquarters.

'It does raise quite the storm of dust, Latimer.' He met Latimer's eyes, and then added defensively, 'Well, it's different for you footloose and fancy-free drifters. You don't have nobody to consider but yourselves.'

'And that's how it's gonna stay if this is what bein' married does to a man. *Whatever you say, dear,*' Latimer mimicked sarcastically.

'Your time just might come . . . ' Jason Kirby shot him a sly, sideways glance. 'But not here, I don't reckon.'

'Meaning what?'

'Meaning, you're likely wastin' your time settin' your cap at Narcissa Filmore's daughter, Tara.'

It seemed to Morgan Latimer that everybody in town was under the impression that he had gone stark crazy over Tara Filmore, just because he had paid her a little attention. They didn't know this drifter. To Morgan Latimer, freedom was the most important aspect in his life.

The second most important aspect at the moment was cash.

'I'd like to enter the race,' Latimer boldly confided. 'But I can't afford a wagon.'

Jason Kirby shook his head regretfully. 'I'd like to help you, son, because I reckon you've got the gut-stuffin' to make a good driver. Too bad I can't do nothin'.' He sighed. 'Anyway, you'd only lose. I expect to set a race record this year.'

'If you win, you mean,' Latimer grinned.

'No question about that. But there's $50 second prize. That should tide you over, Latimer.' Kirby shot him another wink. 'Buy that Filmore gal some pretty dresses, huh?'

'Your husband's a topnotch driver, ma'am,' Latimer said as he jumped down from the wagon at the house. 'His big trouble is he talks too much.'

'I've been telling him that for years,' said Mrs Kirby, a no-nonsense type. 'Come on in and have something to eat, Mr Latimer. You look like a man who could use some fattening up.'

Over the meal, the conversation ranged over the race, the feud, Latimer's experiences since coming to the area, and finally his decision to stay on a while if he could find a job. And that raised the subject of Russell Denson.

'If anyone can find you something hereabouts, it would be Denson,' Mrs Kirby opined, 'although he's not famous for his generosity.'

Latimer pointed out that he was looking for employment, not charity.

'Denson's a pilgrim who hates doin' anythin' for anybody,' Jason Kirby declared, accepting seconds from his wife. He attacked the hot food with knife and fork. 'The trick is to offer him somethin' he wants in return, and then he might do somethin' for you.'

'What could I offer a man like Denson?' Latimer wondered.

Kirby considered. 'Too bad you ain't hit it off with that gal's mother . . . ' he said as though thinking aloud.

Latimer frowned. 'Narcissa Filmore?'

'Yep, that would be her.'

He looked from one to the other. 'What's she got to do with me lookin' for a job with Russell Denson?'

'Why, you sure can be dense from time to time,' Kirby said. 'Denson's sweet on Narcissa, of course,' he added triumphantly. He gave Latimer a nudge. 'Didn't I tell you I know more straight-out, lowdown, hen-scratch gossip than any other ten men in the Mission Valley? Pays off sometimes too. You got to take advantage when you know things like I know.'

'They call it nosiness,' his wife said with a snort of laughter.

'I still find out one hell of a lot, don't I?' Kirby retorted, and after his lady was obliged to agree that this was indeed the case, 'nosy' Jason Kirby told Morgan Latimer the story about Russell Denson and Narcissa Filmore.

Latimer wasn't much interested. But all the talk of the Filmores made him want to see Tara again, and he decided it was time he took the bit between his teeth and rode down to the McKelligon Canyon.

The Kirbys advised against it, but he had never been much for listening or heeding advice.

★   ★   ★

A mile from the house where lush grasslands fringed the stone toes of a crumbling old butte, and elm and oak trees grew heavy, thick and ancient, the long-legged drifter and the girl with the violet eyes strolled through alternating patches of sunlight and shadow in the late afternoon.

It was peaceful here, surprisingly so for the headquarters of a family at war. Latimer had found the Dukes' compound on the other side of the valley to be more like a squat fortress, but the Filmores lived down here in some style, surrounded by rolling parklands and with little evidence of the feud to be seen.

A lone grey coyote watched them from a hilltop before loping away, presumably to look for his dinner.

'That's Gunsmoke,' Tara remarked. 'He's been killing our calves and chickens for as long as I can remember.'

This sounded odd to Morgan Latimer. 'Why doesn't one of your brothers shoot the beast?'

'Too busy shooting the Dukes, I suppose,' came the reply; it had come too nonchalant for Latimer and put an end to that topic of conversation.

They sat side by side on a big log to drink in the beauty of the valley afternoon and talked of unimportant things. Tara looked sleek and lithe in tight-fitting riding pants and a light blue shirt. It had been her idea to take a walk and Latimer rightly suspected that she wanted to get him away from the house, her mother and her brothers — particularly her mother.

The couple couldn't be seen from the house, but were subject of a serious conversation between Narcissa Filmore and her twin boys who stood by the bunk house. Although both were hard cases in the truest sense of the word, Theo and Garrett weren't too bothered by Latimer's interest in Tara. In the wake of Marcus Fowler's death, they felt they had more important things to worry about, yet the matter was of keen concern for their mother.

'I don't like this man,' Narcissa stated clearly. 'He reminds me of a Duke.'

'He's not that bad, Ma,' Theo argued.

'He's a no-account, drifting saddle tramp!' Narcissa contented.

'Tara knows how to deal with the fellers, Ma,' Garrett said mildly. 'I don't see what you're getting into a twist about.'

'Somebody has to worry about other things hereabouts besides fighting the Dukes,' Narcissa retorted, pacing furtively before her sons. 'She should have sent him packing when he showed up. Why didn't she? Can anyone tell me that?'

Garrett tried to make his reply seem light. 'Heck, Ma, all women don't hate men like you do.'

Narcissa Filmore flinched as though struck. She was hurt by the words, and yet they were true enough. The iron had entered her soul when her husband had died young, leaving her with four children to rear and a ranch to run, along with the legacy of a bitter blood feud to fight. She was a woman who needed a man, but the responsibility of coping alone had endowed her with a lot of male qualities.

It was true she was not interested in romance. It may also have been true that she didn't want it for her daughters either.

'I have no intention of standing by and watching Tara throw herself away on a saddle tramp,' Narcissa snapped. She stood before the twins, rigid and commanding. 'Can I rely on you two to get rid of him, or must I get somebody else?'

Across the ranch yard, the Giant, cousin Jasper Hammond and several hands were unloading a dray. They would do anything that Narcissa Filmore ordered them to do.

Theo sighed windily. 'Can we wait until they come back at least?'

Narcissa hid her triumph. 'Of course,' she said, turning towards the house. 'There's no great urgency. Just see that he leaves, that's all.'

'Tough woman, your mother,' Garrett Filmore drawled.

'So's yours,' Theo replied.

The sun was sliding low, filling the canyon with shadows as the brothers rolled cigarettes and waited.

Down canyon, Tara watched the sky and followed the flight of a hawk or vulture. She was not certain, as she talked about the feud and how it had affected their lives.

Morgan Latimer smoked a cigarette and marveled at the clean, clear lines of her profile as he tried to recall if he had ever felt this good before.

A brightly colored bird drifted down the trunk of the tree behind them, cocking its small, pointed head to study them with bright-eyed wariness. Latimer exhaled smoke. The bird dashed back up into the foliage. The shadows were lengthening. It was time to be getting back.

As they followed the course of the canyon stream, Tara said suddenly, 'Why did you come to see me?'

'I'm not sure,' was all Latimer could say in response.

'You don't strike me as a man who'd

do anything without being reasonably sure of why he did it.'

'Maybe I know and just don't want to say.'

'Why are you scared of me, Morgan Latimer?'

'Not of you, but . . . '

'You're afraid you might get yourself trapped somehow?' Tara Filmore prompted when his words trailed off. 'Is that it?'

He halted and turned to face her, unaware that they were now in clear sight of the Filmore ranch. 'All I know,' he said, taking her by the shoulders and drawing her to him, 'is that from the first moment I saw you I've wanted to do this.'

Latimer kissed her.

Her response was immediate, surprising and passionate. She had either played this game before, Latimer remembered thinking, or else she really meant it.

He knew he meant it.

She molded herself against him and

tilted her head back as the kiss continued for a long time, probably much longer than either knew or intended. For them it was bliss, but something else entirely for others.

'Thought you said she knew how to handle fellers?' Theo said tautly.

'Looks like I was wrong,' Garrett muttered, his eyes dark and disapproving.

Boots crunched on gravel behind the brothers as the Giant and his retinue joined them. The Giant, still showing scars from his main street clash with Latimer, wore a scowl as black as the inside of a gun barrel.

All heads turned at a voice from the gallery.

'Well?' Narcissa called. 'What are you waiting for now?'

Latimer heard the call as he and Tara started towards the yard, but he didn't detect the danger in Narcissa's tone or on the faces of the men bunched in the yard just inside the gate. In truth, he wasn't his usual alert self at that particular moment. He was floating along on a feather cloud, which was no way for any tough character to operate in enemy territory.

'Are you glad you came calling now?' Tara was flushed, girlish.

By way of reply, Morgan Latimer smiled and reached out to take her hand, a reasonable enough thing to do under the circumstances one might have thought, but it certainly didn't shape up that way to the dark-faced men waiting for them.

'Saddle tramp,' Theo Filmore said in a grating voice, 'get your dirty mitts off my sister!'

'Now!' affirmed Garrett, and Latimer immediately realized he was in trouble.

Yet again.

16

Morgan Latimer moved towards his tethered strawberry roan, not walking fast, not walking slow. His long arms swung loosely. He was facing his horse, but from the corner of his eye, he watched the men trailing him across the hard-packed sand of the yard. He had sent Tara on to the house, and she had been wise enough to go without making a fuss. He wasn't making any fuss either, even though the Filmores were doing their best to goad him into something.

Two factors were keeping Morgan Latimer cool: Tara and mathematics. He didn't want to ruin his first visit to the Filmore place with fighting, and even if he did, the numbers he had faced would ensure he would lose. How badly he would lose, that remained to be seen.

That tallied up to only one solution: ride away.

'We don't marry our sisters to people who don't treat them with respect in this area,' Theo Filmore said coldly. 'Not like some.'

'No, we've got our own ways,' Garrett affirmed. 'We beat the livin' sawdust out of them.'

Narcissa Filmore called something and Latimer knew she was behind this. She had hated him on sight. She was one tough female.

He reached his horse and slipped the reins from the rail. He glanced towards the house. Tara and her mother seemed to be in the midst of an intense argument. Latimer lifted his foot to the stirrup iron as Narcissa Filmore shouted, 'Show him he's not to come back here!'

A fist struck Latimer in the small of his back. He whirled. The Giant, his face alight with venom, was getting ready to throw another punch.

The smart thing for Morgan Latimer

to have done was to jump astride the strawberry roan and make a break for it. But he didn't. He didn't always do the smart thing. For a man who prided himself on his reasonableness, he had a short fuse.

He hauled off and kicked the Giant in the groin.

The others rushed him. Latimer went back against the strawberry roan's flank and again used his boot to good effect, catching Theo in the chest and sending him reeling. But Garrett Filmore moved like lightning to grab Latimer's extended leg and twist it, bringing him crashing to the ground while his horse plunged off in fright.

'You're no better than the Dukes!' Latimer snarled, springing to his feet as they closed in on him. 'You're all gutless unless you've got a mob to back you.'

Somebody punched him in the mouth. Latimer retaliated with his best ploy, the good old head butting. The recipient was the Giant, who fell flat on his back as though poleaxed.

Latimer was diving at the Giant's prone figure, hoping to get both hands around his throat, when Theo Filmore brought his six gun butt on the back of his skull to send him spinning into blackness.

The last sound Latimer heard as he went under was Tara's scream, sounding far away.

⋆　⋆　⋆

Levi Duke and his dog stood apart from the others from the family compound as they loafed around the front steps of the Silver Dollar, poking fun at Morgan Latimer who was seated in a rocker on the porch.

'You know,' big Grant was saying, 'I thought this drifter was about the smartest-looking hombre I had ever seen when we first met him out by the creek, but I do declare that black eye he is sportin' improves him. He's even better-lookin' than before.'

Immoderate laughter greeted Grant Duke's wit. Naturally, Obadiah, not one to be outdone, had to try to go one better.

'What I like best is the way the bruises on the left side of his mug kinda match up with the ones on the right. He's real stylish.'

Church bells rang to drown out the rough laughter. It was Sunday in the Mesa Valley, the traditional day off for folks to come to town, go to church, get drunk, or just visit with family and friends. The Dukes were in town in numbers, most toting rifles to use within the two precincts.

Latimer fashioned himself a cigarette and counted up to ten — again. He could have done without the Dukes, even though he felt considerably better than he looked. He had to remind himself that he had allowed himself to get drawn into the brawl at McKelligon Canyon the day before, and the least he could do was avoid repeating the mistake today.

'It's a cryin' shame, I say,' cousin Frank Duke said with mock seriousness. 'The way folks seem to take a natural dislike to this man, I mean. As soon as anybody meets him they want to kick his head in.' He clasped a hand over his heart. 'Lordy, I gotta confess I done it myself at Willow Creek, and blessed if I don't feel the urge comin' over me again!'

Cousin Frank was grossly overweight, and when he laughed everything jiggled. This sight prompted the others to bray and guffaw afresh, a spectacle that did nothing for Morgan Latimer, or for Levi Duke, who was still standing with his dog some distance away.

Smaller, but even meaner than his kinfolk, young Levi was in no mood for frivolity, not even at the drifter's expense. Indeed, he strongly felt that his family should be taking everything far more seriously than they were these days — particularly the feud. The Dukes had struck a decisive blow when they had buried Marcus Fowler up to his harmonica, an incident in which Levi had been intimately involved, and which had whetted his appetite for much more of the same.

Levi wanted to go on with it, but the only one he had been able to interest in a diabolical scheme he was cooking up had been fat cousin Frank Duke who, despite his jolly appearance, had the habits and attitudes of a wolf.

Levi patted his dog then patted the satchel between his feet. The satchel contained four sticks of dynamite. On this sunny Sunday, Levi Duke wasn't thinking of spiritual matters; he was wholly preoccupied with the exciting possibility of blowing the Filmores straight to Kingdom Come.

Although Latimer's thoughts were also relatively violent, he wasn't exactly considering bloody murder, despite the Dukes' persistent efforts to provoke him.

Then things suddenly took a turn for the better as Alma Duke showed up, sized up the scene at a glance, and proceeded to send brothers and cousins packing with a string of warm language that left Latimer looking up at her with admiration and gratitude.

'Much obliged, Alma. I'm beholden.'

'Oh, you poor man. Just look at what those no-account Filmores did to you.'

'Fearsome, ain't it?'

'You don't seem too mad about it, Latimer.'

'Maybe I asked for it, goin' down there.'

Alma looked petulant. 'You went courtin' Tara, didn't you?'

He frowned. 'Somethin' like that. Anythin' wrong with it?'

Alma started off along the street. 'Sometimes I reckon I'll get me a husband,' she said over her shoulder, very childishly.

Latimer erased his frown as he leaned back in the rocker. He had never pretended to understand women. It was enough that he liked them: one in particular. He turned his head as the church bells chimed again. The Filmores attended evening service every Sunday. He thought briefly of trying to get to see Tara, but finally shook his head. Not today. He needed time to heal before he faced Narcissa Filmore and her boys again.

★   ★   ★

Levi Duke peered around the corner. It was only about fifty yards to the Filmores' carriage, which was parked in its usual spot in McKenry's lot not far from the church. Nearby, the Filmore horses stood hipshot and patient, tied to the fence.

The sound of a hymn drifting from the church told the Dukes that the evening service conducted by Reverend Uriah Redden was coming to an end.

It was now or never.

Levi opened his valise to reveal the four fat sticks of dynamite and a long, yellow fuse.

'I'd do it,' Levi whispered, 'but it's

too blamed heavy for me.' He squeezed cousin Frank's flabby bicep. 'Lucky you're strong as a horse, Frankie.'

Frank Duke trembled. When Levi had first aired his proposal to take advantage of the Filmores' regular Sunday evening visits to El Paso, and blow them all halfway across the Mesa Valley, Frank had been all for it. Like Levi, he believed the feud had been sputtering and fizzing along indecisively for far too long, and it was high time something dramatic was done to bring it to an end.

Dynamite in the trunk of the Filmore family carriage seemed as good a way as any. With the right timing, they would be able to finish off Narcissa Filmore, her stuck-up daughters, her sons and a whole assortment of Filmore workers and hanger-ons.

But the original plan had been for Levi himself to plant the explosives in the trunk, light the fuse, and then skedaddle. All Frank had expected to do was be there and offer moral support. Now Levi was calling on him to do the dirty work. This was a whole new poker game.

'I'm too nervous, Levi. I might drop the stuff.'

'You nervous, cuz? Not you?'

'Well . . .'

'You're about the strongest Duke I know, Frank. Everybody says so. 'The fat man', folks say, 'he's got guts enough to string a fence.' C'mon, cuz. Don't let the clan clustered around that rig like bees around a honey pot bother you. Just imagine how you're gonna feel when folks are pickin' bits of 'em up in cow yards half a mile away.'

It was a pretty picture Levi painted for his cousin. 'All right, Levi,' Frank sighed, taking the bag gingerly. 'I guess somebody's got to be the hero.'

'And that hero is you,' Levi assured him, patting his meaty shoulder. 'Now, on your way, Frankie. I'll be watchin' every step.'

Levi Duke expelled a huge sigh of relief as the fat man started off along the gloomy alleyway, clutching the bag as though it was filled with glass or eggs. The truth of the situation, as just about anyone who was less dumb than cousin Frank Duke would have realized, was that Levi Duke had suffered an acute case of last minute nerves. He had planned the attack, secured the explosives and attached the detonators and fuses, teetering on the brink of a quivering funk. Luckily, he had included Frank in his scheme, or he might have been forced to call the whole thing off.

By now, Frank was halfway to the carriage. He turned his head to make sure he could see his cousin and didn't see the stone. He tripped over it and screamed in terror as he felt himself falling. The bag hit the ground with a loud thump and Frank Duke vanished in mid-scream.

DUKE, Francis. Very suddenly left us. Beloved son of Jonathan and Hortense Duke of Mission Valley.

Late lamented cousin of Grant, Obadiah, Alma and Levi. 'May the wrath of the Lord fall mightily upon our enemies.' Memorial service at Baptist Church. Wednesday.

The boys were at the table, waiting for their father to join them for the midday meal before leaving for town and the memorial service. The mood was grim. They had lost another man, and everyone was saying Frank had blown himself up while trying to plant explosives in the Filmore family carriage. It was already something of a joke in the hills and valley. It was bad enough to lose a man, but to be made to look stupid in the process was a bitter pill to swallow.

'Here he comes,' said Grant as footsteps sounded in the corridor. 'Hope the old man's in a better mood than he's been in the last few days.'

It proved a vain hope. As Clifton Duke, the patriarch of the Duke family, strode into the room everyone saw his

202

face was as black as thunder. But only Levi felt the old man's wrath when his father came up behind him and swiped him across the back of the head, lifting him out of his chair and knocking him halfway across the table.

In the stunned silence that followed, Levi lay dazed amongst the broken crockery with his father standing back, looking ready to strike him again if he moved even in the slightest.

'What in the name of the Lord was that fer?' Obadiah demanded.

'Why don't you ask your brother?' Clifton Duke snapped, pointing to the dazed Levi. 'Go on; ask him who bought two pounds of dynamite and detonators from Johnson's store last Friday night. Go ahead, ask him!'

Levi stood accused. He knew the jig was up, so he didn't deny it. Sliding back into his chair with blood trickling from the corner of his mouth, he said thickly, 'I dunno why you're so sore, Pa. I wanted to put an end to this here feud. To finish off those no-account

Filmores once and for all. I would have too, if only for that useless fat cousin Frankie . . . '

'How many times do I have to tell you?' Clifton Duke said, shaking his fist at his youngest son. 'Our war is with the men, not the women. You could have blown that woman clear to hell.'

They knew which woman he meant. They stared at him in silence and out of fear, reminded afresh that their tough old pa had his weakness: Narcissa Filmore.

★   ★   ★

Tara Filmore slipped away from the memorial service and made some use of the time to seek out Morgan Latimer, who she finally located in a back room of the town's saloon, drinking whiskey with Jason Kirby.

Latimer greeted her with a big smile, and she was amazed at the transformation a couple of days had wrought in his appearance. Apart from a fading black eye and a couple of healing cuts, he looked just fine, whereas she had half-expected to find him laid up in bed with a doctor close by and a preacher giving last rights to him.

'We've just been discussin' the wagon race, Miss Tara,' Kirby declared after they had made her comfortable and bought her a drink. 'Your friend here's got the notion he can beat me, but I've been tellin' him he's not in the event without a wagon and team. Nice enough feller, but slow to catch my drift.'

'I'm not sure Tara's all that interested, Kirby,' Latimer said soberly, studying her.

'I guess she ain't,' Kirby said, catching that look. He collected his hat. 'Well, I got things to do.' He winked. 'Like trainin' for the race. Put your money on me if you want to show a profit, Miss Tara. See you around, Latimer.'

'So . . . ?' Latimer said after Kirby had left.

'I want you to leave, Morgan,' Tara said without preamble. 'I want you to get out of the valley, heck, the state. Will you do that for me?'

'Hey, this is a bit sudden, isn't it? What's brought all this on?'

Tara explained. She now feared for his safety. Although nobody, apart from Frank Duke, had been hurt in the explosion, the Filmores had interpreted the incident as a grave escalation of hostility in the war, and were gearing themselves for all-out battle. That morning, her mother had said that anybody who wasn't with them was against them, and that included Morgan Latimer. She had come to ask him to leave before he got himself killed. Her reason? Because she cared for him. She was afraid she cared more for him than she really should.

Morgan Latimer didn't know whether to be happy or sad; she loved him, yet was insisting he leave town.

He was considering his next move

when Narcissa Filmore showed up and she wasn't in a good mood.

'I figured you would have sneaked away during the service to this good fer nothin' scoundrel,' Narcissa spat. 'And you've proven me to be right yet again, girl!'

'I didn't sneak off,' Tara shot back hotly. 'I have a right to visit anyone I like.'

'Over my dead body!' Narcissa bellowed.

Morgan Latimer tried to head off the wrangle, but failed miserably. Mother and daughter were both spirited and obstinate. Latimer admired the way Tara stood up to her mother, but sensed that in any serious confrontation between the two women, Tara would back down and lose. Her mother had the power. And as the quarrel continued, he realized Narcissa Filmore was also implacably opposed to romance of any kind, which caused him to speculate that what Narcissa really needed more than anything else was a man in her life and maybe her bed as well.

She was still an attractive female, he observed, taking the opportunity to roll a cigarette while they sorted the situation out, albeit bitterly. Maybe too bitterly to be reclaimed.

He looked at Tara. She had tears in her eyes now. Her mother was getting on top. Latimer felt a sudden pang of guilt. He liked Tara Filmore more than any other girl he had ever known, but he also knew nothing could possibly come of their friendship. He had nothing to offer her. A saddle tramp, drifter, or scoundrel — as Narcissa had called him — on the free, wandering about the West with barely enough money to meet his room rent, was going to be of no use to any girl.

It was plainly time to reach a decision, and he did so quickly. There was no point in beating about the bush any longer.

'Ladies,' Latimer broke in. 'You can stop all this squabblin'.' He looked at Tara. 'I will leave.'

17

Apart from the crashing sounds of a drunk demolishing a trash can outside, it was quiet in the rear alcove of the Silver Dollar saloon where Morgan Latimer sat drinking.

Outside in the alley, his strawberry roan stood saddled and ready with his bedroll strapped across its hindquarters. Following the harrowing scene with Tara, Latimer had said his farewells to Alma Duke and Jason Kirby, the only people in the town who really liked him. When he finished his beer, he would be on his way. To where, he did not know.

He knew he had to leave El Paso or Hell Paso as it was becoming known.

Leave the town and those two families to their feuding, fussing, and fighting, he told himself.

It was a wise decision.

Even if things could have worked out with Tara Filmore and himself, this was still too violent a place for peace-hungry Morgan Latimer.

The alcove curtain was drawn aside and he found himself looking up into the remarkable, bespectacled face of Russell Denson, the richest man in the area.

'What do you want?' Latimer growled. Like most people, he didn't like Denson.

'I understand that you're leaving town, Latimer.' Denson removed his hat. 'May I sit down?'

Latimer grunted and watched the man suspiciously as he slid onto an adjacent stool. What was this moneybags after, he wondered. The Densons of this world didn't mix with the Latimers.

'Whatever it is, make it quick, Denson. I'm about to haul my freight out of this hellish town.'

The light reflecting from Denson's spectacles made it impossible to see his eyes as he leaned back, clasping his hands on the bar before him. He was a remarkably neat, clean man, Latimer noticed. He smelt faintly of lavender water.

'I'm told that the course of true love is running less than smoothly for you, Mr Latimer.'

'What?'

'I've heard about your clash with Narcissa Filmore and your noble decision to quit the town and area so as to avoid further conflict between mother and daughter.'

'What business is that of yours?' Latimer was thinking of what gabby Jason Kirby told him about Denson and Narcissa. He doubted it was true.

'None, of course. Tell me, Latimer, were you serious when you told Jason Kirby you would like to enter the wagon race, but were prevented from doing so by the lack of a wagon and a shortage of funds?'

'You jump around like a cricket on a griddle, Denson.'

'Did you or didn't you? It is a simple question, surely.'

'All right, I did. Now, what business is that of yours?'

'Do you know that the wagon race is a heavy wagering affair? Thousands of dollars change hands on the outcome. I'm a man who's interested in making money, and I would certainly like to back the winning driver this year. Kirby tells me you are a skilled driver. Tell me, Mr Latimer, do you think that if I were to stake you to a wagon, a team and living expenses up to race day while you train and prepare yourself, there might be a reasonable chance of you coming in first?'

Latimer nearly gasped. 'You're pulling my leg. You're kiddin' me!'

'Do I look as if I am kidding you?'

The answer had to be no. Denson wasn't one to joke about the chance at winning money.

* * *

Grant Duke climbed down off the wagon, brushing dust off his clothes as the horses stood blowing and sweating from the hard run to town. He had wheeled into the rear yard of the Silver Dollar, where his father and brothers waited on the porch with glasses of beer or whiskey in their hands.

Grant had thought he'd made an impressive arrival, but his kinfolk looked anything but enthusiastic as he walked towards the saloon in the bright Texas, mid-afternoon sunshine.

'I've seen faster flies in molasses,' was Clayton's uncomplimentary offering.

'Flies in molasses wearin' hobnailed boots,' Obadiah amended, feeling that he had to go one better.

Levi said nothing, having grown very subdued since the dynamite incident and the death of his cousin Frank.

Clifton Duke, also strangely silent these days, just took his pipe from his mouth and shook his head.

Plainly, nobody was impressed with Grant's prospects of winning the town's wagon race.

'Nothin' like some encouragement,'

he muttered, and shouldering past his kinfolk, went inside to buy himself a drink or two.

It wasn't usual for the Dukes to be in town en masse on a weekday, but things were far from usual the past week. The botched dynamite incident had not only cost the Duke family a relative, it also cost them a bunch of respect, but had also succeeded in putting their enemies on full alert. Everyone was now living in prickly anticipation of what some were already referring to as 'the final showdown'. It was a foregone conclusion that the lid would soon be blown off, but nobody, not even the Dukes or the Filmores, seemed to know when or where this would occur.

'I'm gonna win that darn-blamed $500 come hell or high water,' Grant vowed over his foaming beer. 'I needs that money.'

'We all needs that money, you mean,' his father corrected. The Dukes were straining to make ends meet. You couldn't run a spread like theirs or fight a war as they had been doing. The bank was making threatening noises about overdue payments. There was some comfort in knowing that the Filmores might be in even more dire straits, but not much.

'I'm growing weary of being poor,' Obadiah said heavily, staring from face to face of his kin. 'And as far as I can figure, there is only one way out. Finish off the Filmores once and for all, then git back to workin' our land all properly — like we should be.'

'Damn right,' Clayton agreed. He looked to Levi for support, but the formerly outspoken young man was pale and silent. It was possible that the unforgettable experience of seeing cousin Frank Duke being blown to smithereens when the dynamite had been prematurely detonated, had sapped young Levi's spirit and forever scarred him in unseen ways. So Clayton turned to his father. 'What do you think, Pa? Don't you agree?'

'The day I start agreein' with

anything a halfwit like you says I'll know it is time to throw me in a box and bury me underground!' came the caustic reply.

This was typical Clifton Duke — sour to everybody and meaner than a rattlesnake, mostly to those closest to him. Yet it was all show, for this old hill man had, of late, taken to moping about the Duke compound, alone and withdrawn, plagued by uneasiness. It was almost as if he was tiring of the good things in life, such as shooting people and hating everything that wasn't named Duke. Instead, he found himself dreaming wistfully of such things as a pipe and slippers before a nice fire and even — perish the thought — a woman to make it all the more comfortable.

Clifton Duke thought he must be coming down with something. Was he losing his mind? Either that or he was getting old and soft and weak; he didn't know which would be the worst.

Shouts sounded from the street and

Filmores a finishir
got in first and fi
Clifton Duke wh
give the matter i
ation. Yet through
followed, the Du
acted as though hi

Grant, Obadiah
worried about th
father, and as well,
getting the Film
problem was how.

Word had it th:
was now keepin
McKelligon Cany
There was even an
that as well as havi
keep unwelcomed
Filmores were keep
in — namely Ta
Narcissa Filmore
daughter associatin
Latimer.

The Dukes didn'
this was true. The
sure of was that th

the customers went out front to investigate. With nothing better to do, the Dukes joined them and saw a pair of racing wagons come hurtling in off the flats with the drivers standing on their rigs, cracking their whips.

'Kirby and Latimer!' a porch loafer said. 'Just look at 'em go, will you!'

The drivers were going all right; they were burning up the street. The Dukes had heard that Morgan Latimer had somehow got hold of a wagon and team to enter the wagon race, but this was the first time they had seen it.

'Couldn't drive a nail, either of them,' was Obadiah's sour comment. He gave Grant a nudge. 'Hell, I reckon even you could beat those two.'

This was meant to encourage Grant Duke, but it failed to do so. He knew that Jason Kirby was favorite for the race, and from what he had already seen of Latimer, he wouldn't be far behind.

The racing wagons hit the next street and came hurtling towards the saloon.

There was a re
them, billowin;
sky, and thicke
from the poun
wheels. The tv
laughing, hittin;
together neck ;
brakes together
and fishtailed ;
main street as t
'Glory be!' a
drifter drives as
'Beginner's
Duke. 'Anyway.
no-account sad
hold of such a
what I would lil
'Most likely h
Obadiah. 'Any'
reached for the
'We got more im
about today. Ri;
The others ;
breakfast at the
had been agree
seriously consi

a death blow to the Filmore clan seemed to be slimmer than ever before. And Clifton Duke wasn't making it any easier by insisting that, under no circumstances, was Narcissa Filmore to be hurt.

'I reckon the old man's crackin' up,' Clayton said later.

'Iffen he does, I'm the one who will take over,' Grant replied.

The only law amongst the Dukes was that of a wolf pack mentality.

★ ★ ★

Alma Duke and Jasper Hammond, kin to the Filmores, met secretly, which was the only way members of the warring clans dared to meet. The venue was the home of one of Alma's girlfriends in El Paso, whom Alma had asked to stay around to act as chaperone in case Jasper got fresh.

Jasper Hammond would have dearly liked to get fresh, despite the very obvious risks. He had always been sweet on Alma, but she had only just begun to return his interest. He suspected Alma had fallen for Morgan Latimer, then had turned to him on the rebound when the drifter had flown the coop. Jasper didn't mind if he was her second choice. He would take Alma Duke any way he could get her.

'When are you fixin' to name the date for us, Alma?' Jasper asked presumably.

'Not until this war between our two families is over,' Alma said casually.

'I wanna marry you this century.'

'Then you'll have to help me bring the feud to an end, Jasper,' Alma replied.

'Why don't you try somethin' easier? Like jumping to the moon?'

'Seriously, Jasper, I'm worried about my folks. I think they're planning something big.'

Jasper ran fingers through his hair then shoved his hands in his trousers pockets.

'I know,' he sighed. 'They're the same

down at McKelligon Canyon. Twitchy as hell and jumping at every noise. Them idjuts with that dynamite got everythin' stirred up. I hate to say it, Alma, but your pa's got a lot to answer for.'

'It wasn't Pa, it was Levi.'

'Danged young Levi.'

'That's no help, Jasper. What are we going to do?' she asked.

'We could run away. You know, elope,' he tossed out.

'I'm not running away, Jasper. If I marry you, I'll do it right here in front of everybody, and your family and mine can like it or do something else. I rightly don't care anymore.'

'You're gritty, Alma. Y'know, I reckon you've got a fair bit of Duke in your makeup.'

Alma was furious. She stared at him. 'A fair bit? I'm all Duke!'

That, brooded Jasper Hammond, was a disturbing thought.

18

Narcissa Filmore hated bookwork. She believed she was better suited to riding the range or dealing with recalcitrant daughters. Yet these days, more and more of her time seemed to be devoted to accounts and figures — mainly because the Filmore clan was slowly but surely going broke.

At the second round of voices, Narcissa glanced up from her desk to see her daughters stroll by on the gravel drive, Lena smiling and happy, Tara tense and resentful-looking as she glanced towards the house.

With a sigh, Narcissa set her quill aside and got up. She hated being forced to keep Tara confined to the canyon, but it was for her own good. Morgan Latimer had decided to stay on in the area, ostensibly to take part in the wagon race, but Narcissa Filmore believed his real reason was to pursue her daughter. It had been the realization that Tara apparently returned the drifter's feelings that had prompted Narcissa to confine her to the ranch until Morgan Latimer was long gone.

Morgan Latimer . . .

Narcissa hated the sound of that name. Long, lean Latimer reminded her too keenly of her husband for comfort. Narcissa had felt betrayed by her husband's early death and had not trusted any male since. She had smelled trouble in Latimer from the outset, and he had certainly caused his fair share to prove her right. He was responsible for a rift in her family, and to cap things off, was now regarded as a strong contender to win the wagon race.

She hoped Theo would win the race, of course. They needed that prize money, without a doubt.

Narcissa returned to her desk to stand frowning down at the rows of figures that spelled out the swift decline of McKelligon Canyon's fortunes. These days, they were spending more on funerals than on stock feed. Ammunition was another big item. She knew she might be able to get her nose in front if it had been possible to switch even half her men from sentry duty to cattle work, but she dared not. Theo and Garrett believed the Dukes were plotting something big, and Narcissa shared their fear. This meant the spread must remain on full alert indefinitely.

The letter in the small steel rack on her desk caught her eye. Narcissa picked it up and tapped it on her fingernail. Denson's latest offer to bail her out of trouble had been delivered by hand just that morning. She would reject it as she did all the others, of course. No Denson offer came without strings. She would rather bed down with one of her bulls, or even — perish the thought — with Clifton Duke.

Narcissa ran her fingers through her graying brown hair as she moved about the room thinking of Clifton Duke, known to be a ruthless, uncaring and sorry excuse of a father. She half-smiled as she thought about the last time they had seen each other. It had been quite pleasant, really; she had almost forgotten, as they shared coffee and cake, that he was her enemy and, given half a chance, would shoot her down in cold blood without a moment's hesitation.

She went outside, suddenly needing fresh air.

The Filmore house was one of the finest in the region, and was Narcissa's great pride. It was a spacious building, with plain white walls, under a low-pitched roof and a deep gallery across the front. The biggest live oak in the valley shaded the eastern windows, and rambler roses climbed, unhindered, along the gallery.

Just looking at her house brought Narcissa Filmore comfort, although today she was beset by a treacherous thought. She wondered what it would be like to again share it with somebody who was not a son, daughter or employee. Someone to lean on . . .

She was angry as she returned inside the house. It was coming to something, she thought closely, when you could not even trust your own emotions.

* * *

Russell Denson's house, part of the Golden Plume Ranch, was much like the man who lived in it — cold and colorless, with each room containing the minimum of expensive furnishings, bare polished boards and no flowers or ornamentation.

Morgan Latimer noted the military orderliness. Somewhere in Denson's past, there had been some soldiering. He felt sure he would have been an officer. It was difficult to envision even a youthful Denson taking orders.

Denson's ranch foreman, Ambrose Orton, had shown him into the front room, then briefly left before returning with a glass of whiskey.

'Mr Denson will be with you in a

minute, Mr Latimer. Take a seat if you like.'

Latimer did so. The chair was hard. Ambrose Orton didn't leave the room, but stood by a window with his hands linked behind his back. Latimer sipped his whiskey and asked, 'Chased any women into creeks lately?'

Ambrose Orton flushed. The Alma Duke incident had been one of the less illustrious episodes of his career, and he preferred to forget it. He remained silent, so Latimer tried another track.

'What's it like to be someone's flunkey, Orton?'

'I now understand why you don't have many friends, Mr Latimer. I can see why they hate your guts.'

'That's better, man. I get sore when people clam up on me. So now we're talkin', why don't you tell me why Denson sent for me?' Latimer asked.

'I don't know.'

'You're better at molestin' women and scaring them half to death than you are at lying.'

At that moment, Denson strode into the room. Dressed all in gray, he looked thoroughly bleached out and unimpressive. He greeted Latimer perfunctorily and took a seat, waving aside Ambrose Orton's offer of a drink.

He had some grave news, he advised. He had been informed that Tara Filmore was being held against her will at the McKelligon Canyon ranch because of her association with Latimer. Further, he believed her general condition was deteriorating as a result of her treatment and confinement.

His words brought Latimer to his feet. He had wondered why he had seen or heard nothing of Tara in days, and had feared it might have something to do with him.

'Why are you telling me this?' he wanted to know, even though he had no reason to doubt Russell Denson's word.

'I feel we've become friends, so I thought you should know,' Denson offered.

'I'm goin' out there,' Latimer declared grimly.

★ ★ ★

When the sheriff saw Morgan Latimer emerge from the hotel wearing a grim look and toting a rifle, he felt a deep twinge of unease. It seemed to him that the lean drifter had, either directly or indirectly, been involved in every incident that had caused Abel Stark to sprout a whole new crop of gray hairs over the past ten or so days. And just in case Latimer was figuring to start more trouble now, the lawman walked across to the hitch rail. He reached him just as he was preparing to mount his strawberry roan.

'Nope,' Latimer replied to his query. 'No trouble, Sheriff. Just goin' out to hunt some rabbits at sundown.'

'You look ornery, Mr Latimer,' the sheriff noted.

'That's just my nature,' Latimer shot back. 'Besides, this town has made me more ornery.'

'You've got somethin' bulging in your jacket pockets. Looks like boxes of

230

shells to me,' the sheriff said.

'You need shells to hunt, don't you, Sheriff?' Latimer replied, poker-faced.

Abel Stark frowned. 'I don't like you much, Mr Latimer.'

'Who in the hell does?' Latimer said with no emotion. 'Feeling is mutual, Sheriff,' he added.

Stark was getting nowhere, so he just sighed and waved Latimer on his way.

As the drifter rode out, taking the south trail, Ambrose Orton stepped from the store across the street to watch him disappear before striding to the Silver Dollar Saloon to look up Clifton Duke.

He located the head of the Duke family seated alone, hunched over a glass of whiskey, at a rear table watching his sons playing billiards. Naturally, the brothers were arguing bitterly; it was the only way they knew how to play. It struck Ambrose Orton as curious that Clifton didn't seem to be enjoying the fight as much as he should, or normally would have. He looked tired, he thought. Maybe, came the hopeful thought, the rotten old man had something fatal.

'Mr Duke,' he beamed. 'You know me, don't you?'

Clifton Duke fixed on him with a bleak eye. 'Uh huh. You're Denson's roustabout.'

'Well, I'm a bit more than that . . . ' Orton began, and then broke off. Don't waste time, he told himself. Do what you're supposed to do, and do it quick. Tell the old polecat that Morgan Latimer has gone off to McKelligon Canyon to hatch up an anti-Duke plot with the Filmores. Denson said he would swallow it, so try him out.

Clifton Duke believed Orton. Throughout his long day spent in town, he had been waiting for some sign that the enemy was on the move. His every instinct told him it was in the air, and this new information from Orton sounded exactly like the sort of thing he had been expecting.

'That long piece of trash has been

against us Dukes right from the start,' Clifton Duke said menacingly. He frowned suddenly. 'How do you know he's gone to McKelligon?'

'You don't have to believe me,' Ambrose Orton said off-handedly. 'You can just sit here and watch your boys fool around until the Filmores set fire to this dump, or whatever else they will cook up with Latimer.'

Clifton immediately summoned his sons and passed on the news. The result was better than Ambrose Orton had hoped. Even before he left the saloon, he heard the Dukes planning to ride to the canyon to nip the 'Latimer-Filmore' plot in the bud. And he heard big Obadiah saying, 'I knew Latimer favored the Filmores all along. We should have nailed him the first time we caught him molestin' our sis out at the crick.'

'Ain't too late,' Grant replied.

Gaining the porch, Ambrose Orton paused to wipe his brow. Working for Denson paid well, but it was risky business.

He enumerated on his fingers what Denson had told him to do: first, send a rider to tip off the Filmores that they could expect trouble. Done. Second, make sure Morgan Latimer headed for McKelligon Canyon. Done. Third, tell the big lie to the Dukes and make sure they act on it. Done.

Now to get back to Denson and try to find out just what it was all about.

Meantime, out back, a wide-eyed Alma, whose return to the saloon from her illicit visit to Jasper Hammond had gone unnoticed by her family, stood behind a partially-open door listening to her father and brothers talk in heated, low voices about the Filmores and Morgan Latimer.

★   ★   ★

Had either Denson or Orton been expert sign readers, they would have been able to tell which hoof prints were Latimer's, which were Alma's, and which were the Dukes' as they followed the trail towards McKelligon Canyon in the early twilight. But as they were not, their only assurance that their plans were going according to schedule, was the cloud of dust up ahead left behind by the Dukes, who had headed south, without knowing Alma had preceded them.

Riding in his handsome surrey with Orton driving, Denson rubbed his hands together in nervous anticipation. The rich man was sweating in his conservative gray suit. Mostly, Denson pulled strings from a safe distance, but tonight he wanted to be personally involved. This was to be the big night. Everything for which he had been working for so long was to be resolved tonight. By this time tomorrow, he could have everything he wanted.

Yet he still had not told his right-hand man what he wanted to know.

'I like working in the dark,' Orton said sarcastically. 'I mean, just because a man could be risking his life doesn't mean he should know why, does it?'

Denson relented. He realized he had been playing his cards too close to his chest for so long that secrecy had become an obsession. Now that the end was in sight, he felt he could afford to loosen up some.

'Well, surely you can see what I'm doing tonight, man?' he said.

'Of course I can. You're cooking up a showdown. Any fool can see that. But why Latimer?'

'Latimer was a stroke of luck,' Denson confided. 'I needed a tool to help me bring the feud to a head. The drifter just happened along at the right time. He antagonized both families, and both believed he was in cahoots with the other. That's why I kept him here when he planned to leave. I knew I would get the opportunity to use him to good effect, and it has come today.'

'OK, so that explains Latimer. But what about you and the feud? How come you've been keeping that pot boiling? How come whenever the fighting's begun to fizzle out, you've moved in to fan the flames? I've seen you do it time and time again. If the Dukes look like losing interest, you get me, or one of the boys to do somethin' to them that they will blame the Filmores for . . . and it starts up again. Same with the Filmores. It is you who has kept the feud on the boil more than anyone else, boss, and I'd sure as hell like to know why.'

Denson hesitated. It was hard for him to come clean, yet conversely, he now felt the powerful need to boast, to let at least one other human being know just how sly, clever and ambitious he really was.

He looked at the sky. The twilight was dying. He felt a surge of excitement, anticipating what the coming night would bring. He almost smiled, which in itself, revealed that he was in the grip of strong emotion.

'It was the only way,' he said mysteriously. 'Prosperity was my enemy; you can't bend people to your will while they have money in their pockets . . . ' His gesture encompassed the darkening valley.

'The longer the feud continued the more settlers left, and the poorer those who remained became. So I made damn sure it was kept alive until virtually everyone was gone but the Filmores and Dukes. Then, of course, I had to keep them fighting tooth and nail so that they would have to neglect their spreads and slide slowly, but surely, towards ruin. Don't you see, Orton? With every ranch that folded and with every business in El Paso that closed its doors, I was getting closer to victory . . . the final victory that will be mine tonight.'

Ambrose Orton's mouth hung open as he scratched the back of his neck. He prided himself on being smart, yet felt little wiser despite what he had been told. It seemed all he had heard, was Denson openly confessing to the controlling role he had played in the feud. Ambrose Orton was still no closer to understanding why.

It was too late in the day for pride, so he asked.

The answer astonished him.

19

The Giant reached the end of his beat on the canyon's west rim and paused to admire the final fading of daylight from the darkening sky. His attention had been once or twice drawn towards the crumbling wall of outcrop, which during the conflagration must have felt the full force of the fiery blast that had swept through the hollow and spent its fury upon it. It bore evidence of the intense heat in cracked fissures and the crumbling debris that lay at its feet.

Breathing deeply, filling his big chest with clean, fresh air, he didn't see the long, lean figure rise from behind the deadfall log at the back of him. He neither saw, smelled nor sensed anything untoward when the heavy steel butt of a Colt .44 crashed down on top of his hard head. Then the Giant was aware of nothing at all.

Holstering his Colt, Morgan Latimer reached down to drag the sleeping giant of a man behind the log, where he tied him up with his own belt and stuffed his bandana in his mouth for a gag.

He stood up and drew a long breath to still the beatings of his heart before disappearing again.

He didn't resurface again for several minutes when he eased out from beneath the elevated meat house which stood on the fringe of the Filmore commune. With rifle in hand and mouth set in a thin, hard line, he made his stealthy way towards the house, making full use of the cover afforded by a parked wagon, the horse corrals, the tack room and a stack of fence posts.

Stars began to wink brightly in the velvet arch of the sky and there was a dim glow above the canyon wall that heralded the rising of the summer moon.

He reached the bunkhouse. Rising cautiously, Latimer looked closely through a window to see several men seated at a table cleaning rifles. There was no sign of Tara. His eyes went to the house. She had to be over there, he reasoned. Narcissa would only be keeping her under house arrest; they would not have her locked up. If they had, he would see that they paid for it.

Latimer was in a dangerous mood. It wasn't just a foot-loose drifter who went snaking through the shadows towards the bright lights of the house, but a man with a mission. He had known for some time that he was in love with Tara Filmore, but it had taken the news that she was being ill-treated to galvanize him into action. He was here to release the woman he loved and take her away, and heaven help anybody who tried to stop him.

He froze. A man was coming towards him. It was too late to dive for cover. He drew closer. It was Garrett Filmore, and he was armed with a rifle.

Tugging his hat down over his eyes, Latimer drawled, 'Howdy, boss,' and as Filmore came within range, let fly with a perfectly timed right cross that knocked the young man out cold.

Latimer was breathing hard by the time he had dragged Garrett Filmore's unconscious form behind the pump. He moved towards the house again, his heart beating so hard and fast he half expected it to burst out of his chest. These men would kill him if they became aware of his presence: they were the enemy. Everyone was his enemy tonight — everyone except for the beautiful Tara.

The first window he reached in the west wing of the house revealed nothing but an empty room. But the next window brought pay dirt. Standing on his toes to see in, Latimer squinted through the window to see Tara seated at a table, sewing by the glow of a copper-shaded lamp.

He rapped on the glass. The girl's dark head jerked up. All she could see was a battered brown hat and a man's face from the nose down. But it was enough, and Latimer would never forget the way her whole face lit up as she threw her sewing aside and rushed to the door.

Moments later, she was in his arms.

'Oh, Latimer, I knew you'd come. I prayed you would,' she cried. But then, womanlike, she swung from one emotion to another, from delight to fear. 'But you shouldn't have come here. They're on the lookout for you and the Dukes tonight . . .'

'And at least we have bagged him,' a voice said from the shadows. 'Freeze, drifter! We've got you dead to rights.'

As Latimer stood rigid with Tara clutching his rifle arm, Theo Filmore emerged from the shadows with a repeating rifle and three armed men. Theo waited until his gun muzzle was resting against Latimer's chest before giving the nod to a man to disarm him.

'You were unlucky, Latimer,' Theo said. 'Garrett was on his way to the stables to meet me when you ran into him. I heard him hit the ground.' He gestured. 'Get away from this piece of trash, Tara.'

But she refused to release her grip. 'I won't let you hurt him, Theo,' she cried. 'You have no right to hurt him. Latimer isn't our enemy.'

'How wrong you are, sis,' Garrett Filmore's face was set in taut lines as he pressed the rifle muzzle against Latimer's chest. 'Tell Tara to leave, drifter.'

'Go straight to hell!' Latimer could feel his spirit ebbing. He had come close to success — but close was not good enough. They had him. He had gambled and lost. He figured his future wasn't worth a hill of beans, and the sudden arrival of Narcissa Filmore on the scene certainly didn't promise any improvement.

'So, the no-account drifter!' she said. Narcissa glared from Latimer to her daughter, her breast heaving. 'I warned you what would happen if he tried anything, my girl. You can't say I didn't.'

'Oh, forget you, Mother!' Tara said

angrily. 'Don't think I haven't seen through all this uproar you have been raising about Latimer. It's not him you hate; it's any man that shows an interest in Lena or me. You're just against all men because you don't trust them or believe in love or anything — '

Narcissa slapped her daughter. Latimer immediately gave the old woman a shove, almost knocking her over. The hammer of Theo's rifle clicked onto full cock, and Tara screamed, fearing he would be shot dead on the spot.

Her cry drowned out all but the sudden rattle of hoofs as three riders came swiftly down off the canyon wall, forcing Theo to switch his attention to the new arrivals.

Everybody stared in surprise as the trio rode into the light; two ranch hands with Alma Duke between them.

'She just showed up out of nowhere, Theo,' a cowboy reported. 'Says she came after the drifter. Says she's got some important news.'

'Oh, Latimer, you're all right,' Alma gasped in relief. 'I was afraid I might be too late . . . '

'You are!' Narcissa hissed, her eyes blazing. 'Theo, lock them up while I decide what's to be done with them. A dammed troublemaking drifter and a Duke on my land together is something I . . . '

'Mrs Filmore!' Alma cried. 'I rode out here to try and head off trouble. Don't you understand?'

'She understands, Alma,' Latimer said. 'She just doesn't care.'

'Hush,' Narcissa snapped back. 'The both of you!' She gestured to her son. 'Theo!'

'Oh, stop acting like a general at Antietam, Mother,' chided Lena, who had arrived to stand beside her sister. She brushed Theo's rifle aside. 'Alma is your friend as well, you know. She's not mad with hate like the rest of her family, or like you and the boys are. If she's come to tell us something, then we should listen.'

Latimer sensed it was a new experience for tough Narcissa Filmore to have both her lovely daughters stand up to her at the same time. Narcissa's eyes continued to blaze, yet somewhat less fiercely than a moment earlier when Latimer was sure she would have shot him dead. She was breathing heavily as she lifted her firm chin to fix Alma with a bleak eye.

'Very well,' she planted. 'Tell us whatever foul Duke lie you've been told to tell us, then I'll have you locked up.' If Alma's story was a lie, it was a chilling one. She said her family was trailing her to the canyon. They believed Morgan Latimer was hatching up something against them with the Filmores, and they meant to knock it on the head right here at the source. Alma spelled it out even more plainly as everyone stared at her in silence. She believed, from what she had overheard at the Silver Dollar saloon, that her brothers and her father intended this to be the final showdown, the long predicted battle to the death.

It was impossible to listen to the girl and not believe her. Alma Duke trembled. There were tears in her eyes. For years, she had been a victim of the madness of the feud, and now it seemed that the madness might overwhelm them all — unless somebody did something.

Morgan Latimer volunteered.

'They might listen to me,' he said, talking straight to Narcissa, 'whereas they won't to you.' He glanced towards the rim. 'Maybe if I take Alma up with me, they will hold their fire until I . . . '

'No, Latimer,' Tara cried, clutching his hand. 'I won't have you risk your life anymore. I just won't allow you to!'

Narcissa Filmore's face twisted as she watched her daughter, saw her tears, felt her emotion. Narcissa had been a girl in love herself a long time ago. She could read all the signs and resented every one of them.

But before she could speak, a warning shot came from the canyon's rim and a sentry rode up in the strengthening moonlight to report the approach of a band of riders. They looked back, and the man claimed breathlessly, 'Like a buncha Dukes!'

'Battle stations!' Narcissa snapped. 'You two take the wall and Theo, I'll let you guard the north perimeter . . . '

'No, Mother, please!' Tara cried. 'Just because these men have come here to start a war doesn't mean we have to accommodate them. We've always done that and there have always been funerals to follow . . . ' Tara whirled at the sound of unsteady footsteps to see Garrett coming across the yard. 'Garrett, I know you're tired of all the feuding and fighting. Won't you try and talk to them? There must be another way out of this other than everyone being shot at all the time. There must!'

'You're tired of this?' Theo said in surprise to his brother. For a moment, he was off guard, and in that moment, Latimer moved like lightning to snatch the rifle from his hands.

'Shoot him!' screamed Narcissa, as he backed up with the weapon. But before anybody could carry out the order, the hard clear sound of a slap echoed across the yard, and Narcissa went reeling backwards, clutching her face and staring disbelievingly at Lena.

'I had to do that, Mother,' Lena said breathlessly. 'I'm sorry, but somebody had to.' With dignity and calm that impressed them all, she turned to face Morgan Latimer. 'You were saying, Mr Latimer . . . '

20

Russell Denson could not believe how quiet it was as they wriggled through the long grass towards the rim of the canyon. He had arrived at McKelligon Canyon, anticipating the thunder of guns and the satisfying stink of blood and gun smoke, but instead had encountered nothing but silence.

In poor physical condition, Denson was panting heavily by the time they reached the rim to stare down at the Filmore ranch — a sight that did nothing towards improving his feelings.

Directly below, a group of Dukes sat their saddles in the bright moonlight, fingering their rifles. Across at the house, there was another edgy-looking group, comprising the Filmores and their crew. But the most interesting group of all was the smallest, and it was clearly visible by the tack room, halfway between the Dukes and the Filmores. It was Narcissa Filmore, Clifton Duke and the lanky drifter, Morgan Latimer.

'I don't believe it!' Denson croaked. 'What the hell's going on?'

He wouldn't have believed it even if they had told him. Latimer hardly believed it himself, even though he was right there on the spot. Somehow, by a combination of firmness, tact, strength and bluff, he had managed to set up a parley between the feud's leaders in the hope of averting bloodshed. Narcissa Filmore's attitude was not promising, but old Clifton Duke's was astonishing.

As unseen eyes peered down from the moon-washed rim, Clifton Duke was making a proposal of marriage.

'It's the only way that it will work, Narcissa,' he was saying, holding his floppy black hat to his chest and for once in his life, not looking full of meanness and hate. 'You and me took our children into this feud and now they're poisoned by it worse than we are ourselves. If we are gonna put an end to it, and if McKelligon Canyon Ranch and the Duke family is ever going to have hopes of doin' any good, we've gotta combine — join up and work together. Gosh darn it, Narcissa, we've scared everybody else out of the valley and hills in the area. We could have it all to ourselves, but only if we can stop this feud, and I mean stop it forever. And I've just outlined the way to do it. I've been thinkin' on this a whole heap for weeks now and I'm beholden to this ornery polecat here givin' me the chance to say my piece. So, what do you say, Narcissa?'

What Narcissa Filmore said was, 'Me marry you?'

Clifton Duke was undeterred.

'Narcissa Filmore, you cared for me once and you know I've always cared for you. But you went sour on all men when your husband died, and that included me. That's when the feudin' started. You wasn't fightin' me, you was fightin' yourself. Well, it's high time you realized you're gettin' on and you need someone to look out for you. I'm that man. I won't say it will be easy or anything, but with your brood and mine, it — '

'But I'll be around to keep 'em in line,' Latimer broke in hopefully. 'What do you say, Narcissa? What have you got to lose? You're not a happy woman, that much is plain to see. And if the choice is between getting hitched and settlin' down, or seein' your family and his go to the graveyard one by one, I sure know what choice I'd be makin'.'

It was something to see, the way Narcissa Filmore's fierce resistance crumbled before their eyes. She might not be about to fall, swooning, on Clifton Duke's breast, but as the moments went by, it grew increasingly plain that the old man's words had affected her. Suddenly, Narcissa Filmore looked like a very tired and very normal middle-aged woman who had glimpsed a ray of light at the end of the tunnel and wanted to see more of it.

'We'll talk to the boys,' she decided finally.

'And your girls,' Latimer added sharply. 'They've both showed tonight they ain't prepared to take a back seat to you any longer, Narcissa.'

'My Alma too,' Clifton Duke said wonderingly. 'Imagine that girl comin' out here the way she done. I tell you, Narcissa, bringin' up this brood needs two parents pullin' together . . . '

It was as the group moved towards the house that Denson tapped his henchman on the shoulder.

'Bring down a Filmore,' he ordered, as simply as if he were ordering a drink at the saloon.

Ambrose Orton stared. 'What?'

'Whatever they're cooking up, we're going to put the lid on it.' Russell Denson was grim-jawed and venomous. 'Shoot a Filmore and they'll think the Dukes did it. That will trigger off the showdown we want.'

'But we're not in a good position here, Mr Denson. We could be seen! We could get sh — '

'Do it, and do it now!' the land baron barked harshly.

Orton's heart wasn't in his work as he drilled a shot at the group before the house. But he brought down the Giant, who was still falling as Morgan Latimer threw his rifle to his shoulder and fired.

Morgan Latimer was the only man in the canyon to see the rifle flash on the rim, due to the fact that he had been looking back, keeping a wary eye on the Dukes, as he escorted Narcissa Filmore and Clifton Duke towards the house. Sighting two figures moving back off the moon-washed rim of the canyon, he opened up with a fierce rolling volley that echoed and reechoed back off the canyon walls. At the same time, he shouted to the scattering Filmore clan and Dukes, 'Hold your fire. This ain't what it looks to be!'

Naturally, what it seemed like to the warring families was that somebody had broken the truce, and it was now open warfare again. But before the guns could erupt, both Narcissa Filmore and Clifton Duke called on their families to hold their fire.

The reason they did so was because, clearer than anyone else apart from Latimer himself, they could see a figure of a man falling from the canyon rim and smashing into the rocks some fifty feet below. While above, the man who had fired the bullet that had wounded the Giant, lay writhing in the moonlight, clutching his shattered and bleeding leg.

★   ★   ★

Ambrose Orton made a full confession while the El Paso doctor was tending his leg. By now, everyone realized that Russell Denson had been somehow involved in the feud. But nobody knew the extent of the involvement, or the reason behind it — with the exception of Narcissa Filmore.

Narcissa was the only one who knew

that ever since her husband had passed away, Russell Denson had wanted her to marry him. And when Ambrose Orton revealed what Denson had told him the previous night, Narcissa, although stunned by the revelation, could accept it.

The story was a strange one, illustrating just how far a man would go for something he wanted. In this case, what Denson had wanted was Narcissa, and to achieve his ends he had planned to reduce her to poverty so that she would have no choice but to accept him, the wealthiest man in the county. To achieve his ends, Denson had kept the feud bubbling and boiling and had, at the time of his death, brought the valley to the very brink of ruin and caused untold hardship and violence in the name of 'love'.

Two men had loved man-hating Narcissa Filmore. Now one of them was dead, but the other's proposal still stood. And while Narcissa still pondered that offer, Morgan Latimer put in his dollars' worth. He was less surprised than the others were, for Jason Kirby had once told him he believed Denson admired Narcissa Filmore.

'There's no other way of guaranteeing peace, Narcissa,' Latimer insisted. 'Besides, I reckon you want to go ahead and marry Clifton . . . like I want to marry your daughter, Tara.'

'And I want to marry Jasper Hammond,' Alma Duke spoke up.

It might have been the logic that reached Narcissa Filmore, or then again, it might have simply been the fact that weddings seemed to be in the air around El Paso. But there was jubilation in El Paso that day when it was made known she was seriously considering Clifton Duke's marriage proposal, and would give her decision following the wagon race.

The wagon race!

Just about everyone had forgotten about that race.

* * *

A nearly forgotten vestige of the area clattered and stomped through El Paso that evening as teams of horses tore around the town at the annual wagon races.

Eight teams — consisting of a wagon, driver, three outriders and seven horses — competed in the regular races. Four teams race at a time. At the end of the night, the two best teams in each heat race against each other.

Each team sets up between two barrels on the infield. Four horses were harnessed to the wagon. Three horses and their riders (the outriders) ride beside the wagon. At the gunshot, the three men on horses outside the wagon throw tent poles and a smoking stove inside the wagon. The drivers then steer around the barrels and onto the track. The outriders hop onto their horses, and it's an all-out dash around the track to the finish line — all in less than a minute and a half.

'You have to get around the barrels and not tip 'em over. Once you get to the track, it's just wide open cruising,' Jason Kirby had told Morgan Latimer.

Maneuvering the wagon was no easy feat, and it can be perilous, Latimer was also told.

'Wagons have been flipped and horses have gone down. It is a dangerous sport. We just watch it and try to be careful,' Kirby said.

The furious race around the track looked anything but careful. It was a flurry of hoofs, clouds of black dust and hats flying through the air to accompany the frantic, straining horses. The outriders urge their horses to catch up with the wagons, to avoid a four-second penalty at the finish line if they are more than 150 feet behind the wagon.

In the end and despite the objections of a sarcastic Jason Kirby, Morgan Latimer won the grand prize of $500.

★　★　★

Tara Filmore was the proudest woman in town when Sheriff Abel Stark handed a sweating Morgan Latimer the trophy and $500 winner purse.

Latimer was proud too, and happy, for it meant he could now afford a real slap up wedding and make a down payment on a nice little spread out along the Rio Grande.

Unfortunately, and despite the fact that they strongly suspected their respective parents would shortly tie the knot, Theo Filmore and Obadiah Duke were less pleased over the result. There had been a large wager on the outcome, and when the two could not agree on the details, the only way to settle the matter seemed to be with fists, boots, elbows and gouging thumbs in the weed grown yard at the back of the Silver Dollar saloon.

Other Dukes and Filmores looked like becoming involved when Morgan Latimer arrived on the scene.

Latimer did not fool around. Using his gun butt, he decked the combatants then fired two shots into the air to disperse the mob that had gathered around. He had a wedding coming up and wasn't about to allow the feud to erupt and threaten all that had transpired the past few weeks.

He had the yard to himself when Abel Stark arrived, dressed for the trail.

'Where are you going, Sheriff?' Latimer enquired.

'Just goin'.' Stark unpinned his badge and handed it to Latimer with a grin. 'Figure, you may be needin' this.'

Latimer looked back with surprise. 'What in the hell for?'

'To help keep the peace around here. Somebody's gonna have to do it and you've shown you're better at it than I ever was or will be. They'll stay peaceable in this valley, but only with someone to crack the whip and make sure they stay in line.' Stark smiled. 'I've quit, my friend. The job's yours, iffen you want it.'

'I don't know, Sheriff,' Latimer replied. 'I've only wanted to find peace.'

Abel Stark shook his head.

'That's the greatest load of hog swill

I've ever heard, Latimer. You keep talking about peace and quiet, yet you've got a natural talent for finding trouble and even more talent for handling it. You were born to fight, Latimer, and the quicker you accept it, the happier you will be.' Stark winked. 'You and your new bride, that is. So long, Latimer.'

It was outrageous, Latimer thought later as he entered the main street. He was a peaceable man. Then he caught a reflection of himself in a store window and saw a long, lean man with a gun on his hip and a set to his jaw that told him the truth.

He was what he was, he realized, not what he tried to kid himself he was. And Stark was right. The valley needed somebody to keep it peaceful. Somebody his size.

He held the star with the thought of eloping and escaping the valley. He was used to running from everything.

Maybe he should follow Stark's decision and ride off further west, away from this potential hornet's nest of trouble.

Yet, there was Tara to consider.

21

His instincts took over and in a matter of moments, he was on his strawberry roan heading west.

Latimer had ridden several miles of sandy desolation before he stopped to reconsider. He had never been called upon to make such a decision as this proved to be. He knew there was little to fear from human enemies, such as the Filmores coming after him for breaking Tara's heart, for they were riding far enough west of the Rio Grande to be out of the path of raiding parties, while this desert country was shunned by Indian hunters. It consisted of sand hill after sand hill, a drear waterless waste where nothing grew, and amid the dread sameness of which a traveler could only find passage by the guidance of stars at night or the blazing sun by day. To the eye, mile after mile appeared exactly alike, with nothing whatsoever to distinguish either distance or direction. The same drifting ridges of sand stretching forth in every direction, no summit higher than another, no semblance of green shrubbery, or silver sheen of running water anywhere to break the dull monotony — a vast sandy plain, devoid of life, extending to the horizon, overhung by a barren sky.

Not long after stopping, night finally closed in, black and starless, yet fortunately with a gradual dying away of the possibility of storms. For an hour, he had been struggling on, doubting his direction, wondering dully if he was doing the right thing and if he was not lost and not just drifting about in a circle. He and his horse had debated this fiercely once, the pony standing dejectedly, tail to the storm, pointing one way and arguing that the wind still blew from the south, and Latimer contending it had shifted into the westward.

He felt lost and uncertain of his location and of his choices.

He had covered ten miles of it by daybreak, his strawberry roan travelling heavily, fetlock deep, but could advance no further. With the first tint of rose in the East, the brooding storm burst upon them in wild desert fury, the fierce wind buffeting them back, lashing his face with sharp grit until he was unable to bear the pain. The flying sand smote him in clouds, driven with the speed of bullets. In vain, he lay flat, urging the horse forward; the beast, maddened and blinded by the merciless lashing of the sand, refused to face the storm. Latimer, all sense of direction long since lost, rolled wearily from the saddle, burrowed under the partial shelter of a sand dune, and called upon his horse to follow him. With his hands and feet he made a slight wind-break, dragging the struggling pony into its protection, and burrowed them both there, the clouds of sand scurrying over them so thick as to obscure the sky, and rapidly burying them altogether as though in a grave. Within an hour, Latimer was compelled to dig himself out, yet it proved partial escape from the pitiless lashing. The wind howled like unloosed demons, and the air grew cold, adding to the sting of the grit, when some sudden eddy hurled it into their hiding place. To endeavor further travel would mean certain death, for no one could have guided a course for a hundred feet through the tempest, which seemed to suck the very breath away. To Latimer came this comfort — he could not advance, then no one else could follow, and the storm was completely blotting out their trail.

It was as if the town didn't want him to leave.

It was three o'clock before it died sufficiently down for Latimer to venture out. Even then, the air remained full of sand, while constantly shifting ridges made travel difficult. Only grim necessity — the suffering of the strawberry roan for water, and his own need for soon reaching the habitation of man and acquiring food — drove him to the early venture. He must attain the Mesa Valley that night, or else perish in the desert — there remained no other choice.

Tying neckerchiefs over his horse's eyes, and lying flat himself, he succeeded in pressing slowly forward, winding in and out among the shifting dunes, with only the wind to guide him. It was an awful trail, the hoofs sinking deep in drifting sand, the struggling horse becoming so exhausted that its rider finally dismounted, and staggered forward on foot. Once Latimer's strawberry roan stumbled and fell on him, hurling him face down into the sand, and he would have died there, lacking sufficient strength to lift the dead weight, but for him finding some hidden inner strength. As it was he continued on blindly, bruised, and faint from hunger and fatigue. He did not speak; he had no breath nor energy left to waste; every ounce of strength needed to be conserved for the battle against nature. He was fighting for life; fighting grimly, almost hopelessly, and alone.

Night finally closed in, black and starless, about horse and rider. Yet fortunately with a gradual dying away of the storm Latimer found more strength. For an hour past, he had been struggling on, doubting his direction, wondering dully if he was lost and merely drifting about in a circle. They had debated this fiercely once, the roan standing dejectedly, tail to the storm.

Some instinct of the plains must have guided him, for at last he dragged himself out from the desert, the crunching sand under foot changing into rock, and then to short brittle grass, at which the roan nibbled eagerly. The slope led gradually downward, the animal scenting water, and struggling to break away. Swaying in his saddle, Latimer let the roan go, and he never stopped until belly deep in the stream, its nose buried. Morgan Latimer shivered in his saddle, until, at last satisfied, the roan consented to be forced back up the bank, where it nibbled at the short tufts of herbage, but in a manner expressive of weariness. Latimer flung himself on the ground, every muscle of his body aching, his exposed flesh still smarting from the hail of sand through which he had passed.

22

Latimer had not the slightest conception as to where he was, except he knew this must be the Mesa Valley still. Utterly confused by the maze of shifting hills, through whose intricacies they had somehow found passage, the blackness of the night yielded no clue as to their point of emergence. The volume of water in the stream alone suggested that in their wanderings they must have drifted to the eastward, and come out much lower down than had been originally intended. If so, then they might be almost directly south of El Paso, and in a section with which he was totally unacquainted. One thing was, however, certain — he would be compelled to wait for daylight to ascertain the truth, and decide upon his future movements. There was another barren, sandy stretch of desolation lying between this isolated valley and that of the Rio Grande or perhaps Willow Creek and his horse would never stand to be pushed forward without both rest and food.

Latimer arose reluctantly, and removed the saddle from the animal, hobbling it so it could graze at will. For a moment, he stared vacantly about into the black silence, and then lay down, pillowing his head upon a saddle. He found it impossible to sleep, the chill of the wind causing him to turn and twist, in vain search after comfort, while unappeased hunger gnawed incessantly. His eyes ranged about over the dull gloom of the skies until they fell again to the earth level, and then he suddenly sat up, half believing himself in a dream — down the stream, how far away he could not judge, there gleamed a steady, yellowish light. It was no flicker of a camp fire, yet remained stationary. Surely no star could be so low and large; nor did he recall any with that peculiarity of color. If such a miracle was possible in the heart of that sandy desert he would have sworn it was a lamp shining through a window. But he had never heard of any settler on the Salt Fork, and almost laughed at the thought, believing for the instant his brain played him some elfish trick. Yet that light was no illusion; he rubbed his eyes, only to see it more clearly, convinced now of its reality.

'All I want to know is if you saw what I saw. That's a lamp shining through a window. What in heaven's name it can be doing here I am unable to guess, but I'm going to find out. It means shelter and food, even if we have to fight for it. Come on, and we'll discover what is behind that light yonder,' he was talking to his horse and that was never a good sign. He must have swallowed too much of the Texas sand.

The light was considerably farther away than they had at first supposed, and as they advanced steadily toward it, the nature of the ground rapidly changed, becoming irregular, and littered with low growing shrubs. In the darkness they stumbled over outcroppings of rock, and after a fall or two, were compelled to move forward with extreme caution. But the mysterious yellow glow continually beckoned, and with new hope animating the hearts of both of them, they staggered on, nerving themselves to the effort, and following closely along the bank of the stream.

At last they arrived where they could perceive dimly something of the nature of this unexpected desert oasis.

The light shone forth, piercing the night, through the uncurtained window of a log cabin, which would otherwise have been completely concealed from view by a group of low growing cottonwoods. This was all the black, enshrouding night revealed, and even this was merely made apparent by the yellow illumination of the window. The cabin stood upon an island, a strip of sand, partially covered by water, separating it from the north shore on which they stood. There was no sign of life about the hut, other than the burning lamp, but that alone was sufficient evidence of occupancy. In spite of hunger, and urgent need, Morgan Latimer hesitated, uncertain as to what they might be called upon to face. Who could be living in this out-of-the-way spot, in the heart of this inhospitable countryside? It would be no cattle outpost surely, for there was no surrounding grazing land, while surely no professional hunter would choose such a barren spot for headquarters. Either a hermit, anxious to escape all intercourse with humanity, or some outlaw hiding from arrest, would be likely to select so isolated a place in which to live. To them it would be ideal. Away from all trails, where not even widely roving cattlemen would penetrate, in the midst of a desert avoided by Indians because of lack of game, a man might hide here year after year without danger of discovery. Yet such a one would not be likely to welcome their coming, and they were without arms. But Latimer was not a man to hesitate long because of possible danger, and he stepped down into the shallow water.

'Come on, Neb,' he commanded, 'and we'll find out who lives here.'

The window faced the west, and he came up the low bank to where the door fronted the north in intense darkness. Under the shadow of the cottonwoods he could see nothing, groping his way, with hands extended. His foot struck a flat stone, and he plunged forward, striking the unlatched door so heavily as to swing it open, and fell partially forward into the room. As he struggled to his knees, the horse's long face peering past him into the lighted interior, he seemed to perceive in one swift, comprehensive glance, every revealed detail. A lamp burned on a rudely constructed set of drawers near the window, and a wood fire blazed redly in a stone fireplace opposite, the yellow and red lights blending in a peculiar glow of color. Under this radiance were revealed the rough log walls, plastered with yellow clay, and hung about with the skins of wild animals, a roughly made table, bare except for a book lying upon it, and a few ordinary appearing boxes, evidently utilized as seats, together with a barrel cut so as to make a comfortable chair. In the back wall was a door, partially open, apparently leading into a second room.

That was all, except the woman.

Latimer must have perceived all these in that first hurried glance, for they were ever after closely associated together in his mind, yet at the moment he possessed no clear thought of anything except her. She stood directly behind the table, where she must have sprung hastily at the first sound of their approach, clutching at the rude mantel above the fireplace, and staring toward him, her face white, her breath coming in sobs. At first he thought the vision a dream, a delirium born from his long struggle; he could not conceive the possibility of such a presence in this lonely place, and staggering to his feet, gazed wildly, dumbly at the slender, gray clad figure, the almost girlish face under the shadowing dark hair, expecting the marvelous vision to vanish. Surely this could not be real! A woman, and such a woman as this here, and alone, of all places!

When she turned, he knew he was safe and the peace he had so long desired had been delivered to him in the form of Tara Filmore.

We do hope that you have enjoyed reading this large print book.

Did you know that all of our titles are available for purchase?

We publish a wide range of high quality large print books including:
Romances, Mysteries, Classics
General Fiction
Non Fiction and Westerns

Special interest titles available in large print are:
The Little Oxford Dictionary
Music Book, Song Book
Hymn Book, Service Book

Also available from us courtesy of Oxford University Press:
Young Readers' Dictionary
(large print edition)
Young Readers' Thesaurus
(large print edition)

For further information or a free brochure, please contact us at:
Ulverscroft Large Print Books Ltd.,
The Green, Bradgate Road, Anstey,
Leicester, LE7 7FU, England.
Tel: (00 44) **0116 236 4325**
Fax: (00 44) **0116 234 0205**